THE NEW ADVENTURES OF SUPERMAN™

EXILE

M. J. FRIEDMAN

BBC BOOKS

Published in the UK by BBC Books
a division of BBC Worldwide Publishing Ltd
Woodlands, 80 Wood Lane
London W12 0TT

First published 1996

ISBN 0 563 40473 6

Typeset by BBC Books
Printed and bound in Great Britain
by Clays Ltd, St Ives plc

*For Charles Ehrlich,
giver of wonderful gifts*

Acknowledgments

The author would like to recognize the efforts of John Betancourt, without whose hard work and diligence this book would not have been possible. Thanks are also due to Mike Carlin, KC Carlson, and Mike McAvennie at DC Comics, for invaluable noodling, as well as Roger Stern for sage advice. Drs. Seth Asser of San Diego and Laurence Glickman of Long Island were kind enough to contribute their considerable expertise. Finally, the author would like to express his gratitude to Charles Kochman, Ann Goetz, and Scott Sonneborn—for giving me this project in the first place, and for displaying exemplary dedication and care throughout the course of the creative process.

PROLOGUE

Thaddeus Killgrave slid back his glasses on his nose, pushed open the door, and strode into the medical theater. He adjusted his white lab coat, which had been specially tailored to his dwarfish height, and pulled his rubber medical gloves more tightly onto his thick, brutish fingers.

Long ago, when he'd been a student at Metropolis's Burnley College, he'd overheard one of his teachers describe him as "Doctor Frankenstein in Igor's body." He chuckled quietly at the thought. It wasn't far from the truth.

After all, Professor Killgrave was all of five feet tall, with pasty white skin and crude, unattractive features. His hair was cut crudely, too, in a bowl shape that he had preferred long before it became fashionable.

The scientist stopped behind a cloth-covered table in the middle of the medical theater. This was it, he told himself. He took a deep breath. Time to put on his showman's cap.

He smiled up at the observation gallery where his audience waited. There, behind a thick glass wall, sat a very powerfully built man who called himself simply "Smith." Not Mr. Smith, not John Smith, just Smith.

The man wore an expensive Italian suit, dark glasses, and several thick gold rings. His short black hair had been neatly trimmed, and his long, slender fingers, steepled carefully below his strong chin, looked elegantly manicured.

Passing him on the street, one might have mistaken Smith for a football player turned business tycoon or a Hollywood movie producer. One certainly wouldn't have recognized him as the leader of a ring of deadly and super-efficient thieves.

Smith's organizational skills, animal cunning, and sheer greed had made him a successful kingpin in nearby cities. But as much as he wanted to, he hadn't been able to gain a foothold in Metropolis.

The problem? Superman, of course. But now all that would change.

Behind Smith were several bodyguards lurking about in cheap gray suits with bored looks on their faces; clearly, this wasn't their kind of setting. They had probably never been in a medical theater before in their lives.

Well, thought Killgrave, he'd give them a show that would command even their attention—a show that would knock their proverbial socks off.

Killgrave lowered the microphone hanging over the table until it was level with his mouth, tapped it twice, and noted how the three henchmen jumped at the sound. He hid a private smile. It must have sounded like gunshots in the observation gallery.

Smith, though, hadn't so much as blinked. A cool character indeed . . . exactly what Killgrave needed.

"Our problem today concerns mice," the scientist said, as though lecturing to a roomful of students. "More specifically, these mice. Behold!"

With that, he whisked away the cloth covering the table, revealing a transparent Plexiglas box. It was divided down the middle.

On one side a perfectly healthy mouse scampered around, looking for a place to hide. Its little pink eyes were bright, and its long white whiskers twitched alertly. On the other side of the box, though, a smaller mouse with reddish-gray sores on its back and scabby bald spots huddled in a corner, shivering uncontrollably.

Killgrave ventured a glance up at the gallery. Smith had leaned forward, his interest obvious. The mice were so small, though, that it would be difficult for him to see anything from so far away.

Good thing I'm prepared, Killgrave thought. *You don't reach the top of any field with sloppy showmanship.*

He reached up for one of the theater's two cameras—and found it was a little too far away. Frowning a bit, he stood on tiptoe, stretching as much as he could. He still couldn't reach it.

Chuckles echoed down from the two-way microphone in the observation gallery. They were laughing at him, he realized with dismay. He was the greatest criminal scientist of his time, and they were laughing!

9

With an effort, Killgrave hid his displeasure; the lowbrows he'd hired to set up the equipment for him must have done it on purpose, to make him look like a buffoon.

He'd take care of them later. This meeting was too important to be wrecked by such a small problem.

Dragging a stethoscope out of his pocket, Killgrave used it to snag the first camera's handle. Then he pulled the handle down and angled it toward the healthy mouse. When he switched it on, a close-up image of the mouse filled the wall behind him.

He repeated the process with the second camera and the sick mouse, adjusting the two images until they were side by side. That way Smith would be able to compare them.

"These two mice," Killgrave said, "are twins. You wouldn't know that from looking at them, would you? No, the one on the right is healthy and strong; the one on the left is sickly and weak. But why? What has caused this sickness? That is the question. Let's take a look."

He picked up a small joystick next to the sick mouse's box. When he touched the activation button with his thumb, a small mechanical device—little more than a hypodermic needle on wheels—approached the sick mouse from the side of the cage.

The little mouse stared at it dully, still shivering. It was past the point of caring, Killgrave thought.

"The needle contains a tiny video camera," he said. "It represents state-of-the-art medical technology. Watch the monitor carefully as I switch over to it."

The image on the monitor showed a close-up of the mouse's fur as the needle approached. As it descended, it showed the creature's pink, mottled skin. Then, when the needle had punctured the skin, the monitor showed the inside of a blood vessel.

Killgrave adjusted his joystick; the image on the monitor now showed blood cells. Then it changed again, showing the inside of a *single* blood cell. It pulsed and heaved, and now and then something grew in it—something that looked like a twisted little ladder.

"DNA," explained the scientist. "The genetic blueprint of life."

Killgrave glanced at Smith from the corner of his eye. The gangster had taken off his glasses and was studying the image closely. His eyes, Killgrave saw, were a piercing gray.

"Chaos," the scientist whispered dramatically. "The sick mouse's blood cells are working to reproduce an incredibly powerful virus—this little ladder, otherwise known as deoxyribonucleic acid, or DNA. In all living things, DNA tells the body what kind of cells to make—cells for blue eyes or brown, big feet or small.

"But in a virus, DNA comprises the whole thing. And its only business is to multiply by forcing itself into living cells and making them factories for more virus-DNA. Of course, the cell is ravaged in the process. And in this case, where the virus is a particularly devastating one, the whole body is victimized. It's completely helpless."

Killgrave repeated the microcamera injection with the healthy mouse. It squeaked and tried to run when the mechanical hypodermic approached, but it couldn't escape. The needle pierced its skin, injecting the camera.

On the viewing screen, the mouse's blood cells appeared red, healthy, and strong. Its whole body surged with vitality.

"This mouse is the picture of health," Killgrave said. "It's hard to believe that only one day ago, the sick mouse looked just like the healthy one. But a day from now, the healthy one will be just as sick as its twin is now."

He pushed a button underneath the medical table, and the plastic divider separating the healthy mouse from the sick one slid down and out of sight. At once the healthy mouse, whiskers twitching, scampered over to investigate its new companion, smelling its breath, touching its skin. And that, Killgrave thought, signaled its end.

"Right before our eyes," he announced, "the healthy mouse's cells will start to change, as they're invaded by this extremely contagious and quick-acting virus. There! You see?"

He pointed to a twisted ladder in the healthy

mouse's blood, which pierced a blood cell, curled up inside, and began reproducing itself. In a few seconds, another ladder emerged to infect other cells.

Killgrave chuckled. He had designed this virus with painstaking care. It was a work of art. Beautiful, even.

"The mouse does not look sick yet," he pointed out. "But as you can see, there's already a discernible difference in its blood cells. The virus has taken root. And once it has done that, it will soon prove fatal. Any questions?"

Smith nodded. "Yeah. I got a question. How is any of this going to help me move in on Metropolis?"

Killgrave frowned. Smith, it seemed, was not a man of sweeping vision.

"This is a highly contagious, highly destructive form of virus I've developed. And," he added boldly, "I plan to infect Superman with it."

"Superman is going to die?" Smith wondered aloud.

Killgrave shook his head. "Unfortunately, no virus alive can kill the Man of Steel. However, he can and will become a carrier of this disease. That means he will no longer be able to appear in public. And if he can't appear in public, he can't stop the sort of free enterprise you represent."

Smith sat back in his chair, a thoughtful expression on his face. He had begun to see the possibilities, Killgrave thought.

"Your people will be able to pull any heist they want," the scientist continued. "They can take over Metropolis. And," he added, "all you've got to do is give me a portion of your take, to fund my further scientific endeavors. Say . . . thirty percent." He shrugged. "It's a small price to pay for what you're getting in return."

Smith's eyes narrowed. "Thirty percent?" he repeated, his voice turning hard and surly. He laughed—a humorless sound. "You out of your mind? Why don't I hand you the whole take?"

"I'm a scientist," said Killgrave, "not a businessman. Let's say twenty-five percent, then, and be done with it."

He didn't really care, of course, what the exact percentage was. More than anything else, he wanted revenge on the Man of Steel.

"Twenty-five?" Smith grunted. "Y'know, I was born at night, but it wasn't *last* night. We're doing all the work, and you want a *quarter* of what we pull down?" He looked at his henchmen. "I don't think so."

Killgrave snorted. "Twenty, then."

Smith eyed him. "Tell you what, little man. I'll give you your twenty. But if it doesn't work like you say, I'm holding *you* personally accountable. And if it *does* work, you owe me."

"Owe *you*?" said Killgrave, finding it hard to keep the disdain from his voice.

"That's right. I get a freebie," the gangster told him. "After all, you're such a big-deal scientist,

14

I'm bound to need you somewhere down the line. And when the time comes, I plan to collect."

Killgrave swallowed his pride. "All right," he said hesitantly. "It's a deal."

Smith nodded. "Good. We understand each other, then. My people will be in touch. They'll take care of everything. Whatever you need, it's yours."

Then the gangster rose and left the gallery without a backward glance. The three body-guards followed, still giving Killgrave suspicious looks.

Philistines, Killgrave thought with a snort. No, worse than Philistines—animals. And he had just made them his partners.

But it was necessary, if he was to make Superman pay for foiling his schemes in the past. And with the Man of Steel out of the picture and a wad of money in Killgrave's pocket, his genius could find its full expression. He could do things other scientists could only dream of . . .

With a sad squeak, the sick mouse expired in its cage. Killgrave regarded it coolly as its legs gave a final spasmodic twitch.

"Thank you," he said softly to the tiny creature, "for your noble contribution to science." Then he began to laugh.

CHAPTER ONE

Lois Lane, arguably the *Daily Planet*'s best reporter, sighed miserably. Some assignments depressed her no end.

She regarded the Big Apricot Health Fair with dismay. Ten blocks of Fifth Avenue had been cordoned off to make room for hundreds of booths, displays, and demonstrations, each dedicated to a different form of health and physical fitness.

Thousands of people had turned out to inspect the latest electronic treadmills, sleek weight-lifting machines, and fancy executive stress-testing units. Thousands more crammed the health food cooking demonstrations, or ogled the attractive young women hopping around in leotards at the aerobics demonstrations.

There were animated exhibits showing the effects of cholesterol on the body and clowns juggling items from all four basic food groups. Beyond them stood rows of book vendors, running-shoe vendors, exercise machine vendors, and health drink vendors.

Everything here was, in one way or another, telling people to take care of themselves. To exercise. To watch what they eat.

And Lois was here with the one person on Earth who could ignore all that—her fiancé, who also happened to be her writing partner. Clark Kent, known to the world as Superman, looked and felt like the healthiest man alive *without* exercise machines and diet milkshakes.

"It's not fair," she said to him for the hundredth time.

Clark looked up guiltily over his glasses as he munched on his third hot dog of the morning. "What isn't?" he asked.

Lois poked her forefinger into his cheek, which was distended with his latest mouthful. "*That* isn't. With your metabolism, you can eat all the junk food you want and never gain a pound from it. But if I so much as *look* at a slice of pizza, I've got to spend the next two days at the gym."

Clark grinned. "At least all your sacrifices haven't been in vain, Lois. You're easily the best-looking woman here. And that includes Priscilla Goodbody."

She eyed him. "Priscilla *Goodbody*?"

He nodded. "The aerobics instructor. Over there," he said, with a tilt of his chin.

Turning, Lois tried to follow his gesture. "Aerobics instructor? I don't see any aerobics instructor."

"She's down that way," said Clark, pointing. "You see? Past the Zip-Ade tent, with those kids around her?"

Lois followed Clark's directions. She squinted and just barely spied the woman in question—a statuesque specimen in Spandex shorts and a midriff-length top, leading a beginner's class of children.

Clark craned to see the aerobics instructor better. "You see her now? The one over there, with the mole on her—"

Lois grabbed his jacket and pulled him to the side. "I think you're paying a bit too much attention to that particular exhibit," she said.

He smiled innocently. "Whatever you say," he told her.

Lois harrumphed. Bad enough there were all these good-looking women around in skimpy outfits. Having a fiancé with telescopic and X-ray vision made it even worse.

Scanning the booths around them, she spotted one that looked potentially interesting. It had a *Newstime* magazine banner overhead.

"Come on," she said, pulling Clark in that direction. "Let's see what the competition has to offer."

With Lois in the lead, they wove their way to the front of the crowd that had gathered around the *Newstime* booth. The magazine was having one of its frequent subscription drives, this time pushing its weekly "Health News" column. And there, in sweatshorts and a tank top, bouncing up and down on a trampoline while holding a microphone, was Keith DeCann, *Newstime*'s muscular health columnist.

"A hundred dollars," Keith was saying, "to the favorite charity of anyone who can meet my challenge!"

"Now this is more like it," Lois observed. She

18

smiled, admiring the man's physique—though it was hard to follow all the bouncing.

"Beefcake instead of cheesecake?" Clark asked, tongue in cheek. He sighed. "I guess what's good for the goose isn't good for the gander."

Lois skewered him with a look. "It's charity work," she said. "You should appreciate it more, considering your own hobbies."

Or rather, those of Superman, she added silently. But Clark knew exactly what she meant.

"Point taken," he replied.

"Hey, hey!" Keith called, hopping lightly down from the trampoline. "I think I see our first contestant!"

He headed right for Lois, smiling and giving her a wink. In the past, he had been a reporter, too, covering the same beats she did, and she'd scooped him more than once.

Was this some kind of revenge? Trying to get her up on that trampoline for a round of high-bouncing—and public humiliation? After all, it was difficult to look dignified with one's arms and legs flailing in the air.

"Come on, Keith, not me!" she said.

Shaking her head, she tried to back away—and ran into Clark, who was standing behind her, blocking her escape. Running into him was like running into a brick wall.

"Be a good sport, Lois," Clark said into her ear. She glared at him, but he just gave her a mischievous look. "It's for charity, after all."

"I know it's for charity, but—" she began.

Keith was right in front of her now. He said, "Ladies and gentlemen—Clark Kent, ace reporter for the *Daily Planet*! Give him a hand, and let's see if we can get him up here to give it the ol' college try! Stop hiding behind the little lady, Clark!"

Clark had clearly been taken by surprise. If Lois knew him at all, he was casting about for an excuse not to participate.

Of course, that wasn't the only part of Keith's remark that she had noticed. "*Little lady?*" she began angrily.

Keith gave Lois another wink and covered the microphone with his hand. "It's him or you," he whispered.

"Take him, he's yours," she said with a grin. "Go for it, Clark."

"Lois!" he protested.

But he wasn't going to get any sympathy from *her*. Not after the way he'd tried to maneuver her up on the trampoline. It was nothing less than poetic justice that Clark should be taking her place.

"Give him a big hand!" Keith cried. "Clark Kent from the *Daily Planet*!" The crowd began to clap and cheer enthusiastically. "Come on, Clark! Don't disappoint your fans!"

Clark looked plaintively at Lois, but she found herself laughing. "Go ahead, Mr. Metabolism," she said. "It's for charity, remember?"

The crowd was still clapping eagerly.

Clark sighed. "What exactly do you want me to do?" he asked in a reluctantly cooperative tone.

"He'll do it!" Keith shouted into the microphone, and the audience roared.

Clark shook his head. How did he get into these situations?

He looked at Lois unhappily, but she was clapping wildly right along with everyone else. There was nothing he could do now but make a show of trying out the trampoline.

Of course, he'd have to fail—just as he'd had to fail at every other physical competition since his powers began to manifest themselves. After all, Clark Kent was supposed to be a mere human—not a super-being from another planet.

"Come on up here, Clark," Keith said, leading the way onto a small wooden stage to the left of the trampoline. He pointed across the trampoline to a high pole, where thirty feet had been measured up from the surface of the trampoline. "See that measuring stick?"

"Yes," Clark said, trying to sound doubtful.

"All you have to do is bounce high enough and you win."

Clark grimaced. "Bounce?"

"That's right. How high do you think you can go?"

Clark shrugged. "Five feet?" he suggested.

"He says five feet!" Keith announced to the

crowd. "Is that high enough?"

"No!" the crowd roared back.

"How about ten?" Clark asked.

"He says he can do ten feet!" Keith shouted into the microphone. "Is that enough, folks?"

"NO!" the crowd roared again. Clark saw Lois shouting, too. She was enjoying this more than anyone, he thought. Of course, she was secure in the knowledge that he'd find a way to keep his superidentity a secret.

Keith leaned closer to him. He put his arm around Clark's shoulder as if they were buddies.

"Clark, my man," he said in a conspirator's whisper, though he was still talking to the whole crowd through the microphone, "you look like the daring type. We want you to bounce high enough so that your head clears the twenty-five-foot mark. Think you can do it?"

Clark swallowed, pretending to be doubtful. Of course, if he wanted to, he could probably reach the moon—but he didn't want Keith or anyone else to know that.

"I'll give it a try," he answered.

"You do it," said Keith, "and I'll see to it that a check for one hundred big ones goes to the charity of your choice. Deal?" He offered Clark his hand.

"Deal," Clark said. They shook on it.

"All right, then," said Keith. "Go to it!"

Clark stepped very tentatively out onto the trampoline. Its taut canvas surface sank a good foot under his weight. Slowly, awkwardly, he made his way out to the middle.

Then he began to bounce. He made a great show of it, flapping his arms and teetering as if he were about to fall, each time just catching his balance. The crowd sighed with disappointment. Clark heard scattered catcalls from hecklers at the back.

"Surely you can do better than that!" Keith called to him, his voice amplified by the microphone. "My grandmother bounces higher than you do, Clark!"

Suddenly Clark shut him out—shut out every noise from the crowd. He had detected something on the periphery of the street fair with his superhearing…

Trouble.

Bouncing higher, clearing all the displays, he strained to see what was going on. Four blocks away, people seemed to be running from something in panic. They were screaming, crying for help.

But he couldn't tell why. Obviously, this was no time for him to be bouncing on a trampoline. This was a job for Superman.

Clark looked down and saw the crowd cheering wildly. He glanced at the measuring pole and saw the reason for it. Without realizing it, he had bounced high enough for his head to clear the thirty-foot mark.

The good news was that he had earned the

hundred-dollar prize for his favorite charity. The bad news was that if he'd bounced any higher, he might have given people cause to wonder.

But the *worst* news was no doubt about to take place in the vicinity of the commotion he'd heard—unless he responded immediately as Superman. As quickly as he could without arousing suspicion, Clark put a damper on his bouncing, rolled off the trampoline, and ducked into the crowd.

His superhearing, focused on the area of the disturbance, told him the screams and cries for help were getting louder, more desperate.

There was no time to waste.

CHAPTER TWO

Lois saw Clark disappear into the crowd, and though she didn't know exactly why, she could guess. Obviously, something required his presence as Superman.

"Well, can you beat that!" Keith DeCann said into his microphone. He was shaking his head and staring off after Clark in bewilderment.

Lois, though, was quick to cover for Clark. She called to Keith, "He's got strong legs but a weak stomach. You should have seen him packing away the hot dogs before you got him up on that trampoline!"

"Have him call me at the office," Keith said. "So he can collect his prize. After all, he earned it." His attention was already moving to his next contestant. "You, sir—yes, you, the bald fellow in the plaid shirt! Are you feeling particularly buoyant today? Care to give the ol' trampoline a try? No? Then how about you, ma'am?"

Turning, Lois pushed her way through the crowd after Clark. If she hurried, she could still be the first to cover the story, and perhaps even beat him to the scoop.

As Clark ran, he bit his tongue in frustration. The crowd was just too dense, the street too tightly packed. It would take him fifteen minutes to travel the four blocks at this speed. There had to be a shortcut, or a place he could hide in order to don his Superman costume.

Everyone was so busy, perhaps nobody would notice if he did it almost literally under their noses. He cast about and spotted a cloth-draped vitamin display table. Ducking underneath it, he found more than enough room to change.

In a matter of seconds, he emerged at the far end dressed as Superman. Moving so fast he registered as only a blur to the fairgoers, he took to the air.

But as he ascended higher and higher, he could see heads turning, fingers pointing, and voices raised in recognition. After all, he was the protector of Metropolis.

"Look, up in the sky…"

"It's Superman!"

His red cape flapping behind him in the wind, he turned in the direction of the disturbance, which he could now see more clearly. It looked like a large dog was running amok—a cross between a Doberman and a German shepherd, Superman thought.

A closer look showed him there was white froth all about its mouth—a clear sign of rabies. The poor animal was howling and snapping at everyone around it, sending them screaming and fleeing in panic.

Not quite the threat he had expected, but a threat nonetheless. Rabies could be deadly, and the crowd could be even more dangerous than the dog itself. There was the danger of a stampede, in which people could be trampled—maybe even killed.

Superman couldn't help imagining the headlines that might result. It wasn't every day you had the threat of death at a health fair.

Of course, the Man of Steel knew those headlines would never appear—not if he had anything to say about it. And he most certainly did, thanks to the yellow sun that gave him his powers.

As Superman descended to Earth, the dog cornered a mother with two small children in a double stroller. Superman swooped down just as the dog leapt at the little girl on his left.

Catching the animal in midair, he carried it up into the sky. Behind him, he heard the mother's hysterical sobbing. There were calls of thanks, as well.

Superman would have acknowledged them with a wave, but his hands were full. The dog, irritated at finding itself in the confinement of Superman's steel-muscled arms, was struggling violently to escape.

But he wouldn't let it move. Not even when its jaws clamped down on his wrist, slathering drool and white foam all over him. Superman sighed and tried to work himself free without breaking the dog's jaw. It had an unusually thick leather collar and dog tags unlike any he'd seen before.

Up they flew, high over the city's skyscrapers

now. The dog began to kick harder than ever, still struggling to get free. Superman swung it around to get a better grip, digging his fingers through its fur and around its wide, heavy collar until he found a nerve center. Suddenly the dog went limp, breathing quietly.

"Good boy," Superman said soothingly. "We'll get you someplace safe."

A moment later, he felt a strange sensation, like ants crawling up his arm. Looking down, he saw that a strange metallic appendage had emerged from the dog's collar and was working its way up his arm.

"What the—?" he began.

Using his X-ray vision, Superman looked inside the device. It seemed oddly complex, full of circuits, gears, and wires. It seemed there was more to this animal than he had anticipated.

But before Superman could act on his suspicion, the appendage whipped around his head and inserted its tip into his right ear.

Something sprayed from it—a spray that penetrated into his ear canal. Then the device tightened around his head and wouldn't let go.

CHAPTER THREE

It was a trap, thought Superman. The whole thing—the rabid dog, the way the crowd could be expected to panic—it was all designed to catch him off guard. And as much as he hated to admit it, it had.

He didn't touch the appendage, even though it was tickling his inner ear. Nothing had really happened so far, and it might have been more dangerous to try to remove it. Right now he had to find out who was responsible—and why they had done this to him.

Using his supervision, he scanned the street fair, looking for anyone or anything out of the ordinary. Unfortunately there were too many people there. He estimated five or six thousand, maybe more.

The culprit had to be watching him, but he couldn't see anyone acting strangely. Even the area where the dog had run wild had returned to near normal.

Then he heard a metallic jingling and remembered the dog's tags. There were two of them hanging from what was left of the collar.

The first one read, *HELLO. I BELONG TO SUPERMAN.* The second one read, *AVOID CONTACT WITH HUMANS. YOU MIGHT BE A CARRIER OF A DEADLY VIRUS.*

Superman swallowed. That's why the appendage had sprayed something into his ear—

someone had been trying to infect him with a disease. But the Man of Steel had an alien physiology. He was immune to every disease on Earth.

But what if they somehow found a way to infect me? he wondered. *What if I really am a carrier of some kind?*

It was a risk he couldn't take. But Superman himself wasn't an immunologist. He was going to need help to find out if he was in trouble or not.

And he knew he could find that sort of help in only one place. Without hesitation, he headed for S.T.A.R. Labs.

From the edge of the crowd, Professor Killgrave watched Superman fly away with the dog. His mechanical device had worked perfectly, injecting its virus into Superman's ear canal. It had been almost too easy for a super-intellect like his to outsmart someone like Superman. He would take brains over brawn any day.

Pulling his baseball cap lower over his eyes, the scientist turned and sauntered away. From all appearances, he knew, he was just another face in the teeming crowds that had turned out for the health fair.

Superman hovered three hundred feet over the front gate at S.T.A.R. Labs. "Hello, you down there!" he shouted to the man in the guardhouse.

The guard wandered out in his brown uniform

and stared up at him, open-mouthed in surprise.

"Superman?" he asked.

"That's right," the Man of Steel shouted down. "Can you call Dr. Kitty Faulkner for me? I have an emergency situation, and I need her help."

Kitty Faulkner was one of the facility's top scientists. She and Superman had worked together many times before.

"Right, will do!" the guard promised. He hurried back into the guardhouse, picked up the telephone, and punched in an extension number.

With his superhearing, Superman was able to hear every word on both ends of the line.

"That's right—Superman! Get Dr. Faulkner out here right away!"

"But what should I tell her?"

"He says it's an emergency. And he's got a dog and something weird stuck on his arm and his head."

A pause. "She'll be right there."

The guard hung up the phone and came out. "They're getting her now!" he called.

"Thanks!" Superman shouted down. "I appreciate it!"

"Hey, you know we'll do anything to help the good guys," the man said.

A few moments later, Kitty came running out a side door. She was a slender woman with glasses and light brown hair. Sizing up the situation, she shouted, "What happened? Can you come down?"

"No!" Superman called. "I'm not sure, but I may have been infected with a highly contagious disease. The dog may have it, too. Can you help?"

"Wait right there!" Kitty called and ran back into the building.

Superman continued to hover in the air. The dog hung limply in his grip.

Kitty came back out five minutes later, this time with a megaphone in one hand and a work crew in bulky white containment suits behind her. They looked a little bit like astronauts dressed for a space walk.

They were carrying a set of large, flexible plastic components. Superman recognized them as parts of a hazardous materials management system that S.T.A.R. Labs had developed a few years back. After all, this facility had plenty of use for it, coming in regular contact with unusual situations.

Quickly, under Kitty's supervision, the men in the containment suits assembled a long, transparent tube, which they connected to a circular door in the building. The other end of the tube had an air lock. Kitty opened the air lock end, then stood back.

"Come down slowly," she said, her voice amplified a dozen times over the bullhorn. "Fly inside. We're setting up a quarantine environment to hold you while we take a look at what you've got."

Slowly, taking great care not to touch the ground, Superman flew into the air lock. He didn't want to take any chances, no matter how slim the possibility that he was contagious.

A man in a containment suit closed the air lock door behind him, then sprayed the outside with some kind of high-tech chemical disinfectant. Walking now, Superman advanced along the plastic corridor toward the building.

Everything around him had been sealed tight. The air smelled of strange chemicals, and the light filtering down through the top of the tube had a milky, unreal quality, which made Superman feel as if he were underwater.

Finally he came to the air lock on the other end. It was open. He went through it into a small room with white ceramic tiles on the floor, walls, and ceiling.

Stainless steel medical equipment was positioned against the wall to his left. The wall to his right contained a metal box, which looked as if it would open from his side. The wall ahead of him was made entirely of glass.

Kitty Faulkner had circled around and now stood on the other side of that glass wall. She touched an intercom button, and suddenly Superman could hear her through a speaker hidden in the ceiling. Her voice sounded flat and far away.

"You can put the dog in the box set into the wall," she said. "We'll examine it in a separate room."

The animal was still out cold. The Man of Steel didn't imagine the lab's scientists would have much trouble with it.

"What about the collar?" he asked.

"I think you can remove it," Kitty advised.

Carefully, Superman unfastened the collar from the dog. Then, as instructed, he placed the dog in the box and closed it up. A moment later, his X-ray vision revealed someone in a containment suit carrying the animal off.

Finally he tore off the metal appendage from his head and arm. It offered some resistance, maybe enough to stymie a normal man. But not a Superman.

"You can put that in the box as well," Kitty told him. "We'll want to get a look at it."

Again the Man of Steel complied.

"Tell me about the dog," Kitty said when he was done. "What do you know about it?"

"I thought it had rabies," he said, "but now I'm not so sure." He told her what had gone on at the health fair.

She nodded. "We'll alert the local hospitals in case anyone shows up with rabies symptoms. What about the appendage? Any idea what it was?"

"No. As I said, it sprayed something into my ear. But the dog's tags held a message warning me that I'd become a carrier for some deadly virus."

Kitty nodded. "I'll have to run some tests on

34

you. I know you have a lot to do, but this may take some time, depending on what we find."

"How long?" he asked tersely, thinking of his job at the *Daily Planet* . . . not to mention Lois and his parents, who would be worried sick if he didn't contact them soon.

"I'm not sure," she said. "I've never diagnosed an alien like you before. But we'll do our best."

Sighing, Superman looked around for a place to sit. The room didn't have any furniture, so he crossed to the wall and sat down with his back against it.

"Do you need anything?" Kitty asked.

Superman raised an eyebrow. "How about a chair, for starters?"

"Sure," Kitty said. "And I'll get you a hospital gown. We'll need to irradiate your clothes." She seemed to think of something problematical. "Er—they're not going to react strangely to the radiation, are they?"

He smiled, despite the circumstances. "No, they're not. They're just made of plain fabric. Nothing alien or unusual about them."

"Good. I'll see if I can find you some reading material as well. It'll keep you from being *bored* to death."

The Man of Tomorrow appreciated the irony. After all the superhuman feats he'd pulled off since coming to Metropolis, all the deadly threats he'd faced down, being bored to death had been the least of his worries.

"Anyone you want to contact?" Kitty went on.

Superman weighed the possibilities. If he took the scientist up on her offer, he'd be taking a chance on revealing his secret identity.

Unless he contacted Lois. It was already well-known that he and the reporter were friends of a sort. But then he would be pointing up the absence of Lois's writing partner, Clark Kent.

Besides, he wouldn't know what to tell her. The jury was still out as to what had happened to him—if anything.

"Not just now," he replied.

"Let me know if you change your mind," Kitty told him. She pointed to a tiny grid built into the wall on Superman's left, right near where it met the transparent barrier. "That's an intercom and call button. You know what to do if you need anything else."

"Thanks," he told her.

She looked at him sympathetically. "Try not to worry, all right? I think it's very unlikely you've been infected with anything. These are just precautions."

"I understand," he told her.

Truthfully, she had brightened his spirits a bit. But the Man of Steel was still worried. After all, someone had gone to a great deal of trouble and expense to spring that trap on him.

And now there wasn't anything he could do except sit helplessly . . . and wait.

CHAPTER FOUR

Lois was having a hard time concentrating.

Sitting at her desk in the *Daily Planet* offices, proofing the story about Superman's appearance at the health fair, she couldn't keep her mind from wandering.

Where had Superman gone in such a hurry? And what was that strange thing she'd seen wrapped around his head?

She knew it had to be something serious. Normally Clark would have phoned her by now just to check in. She had begun to get more than a little worried.

"Hey, Lois," Jimmy Olsen said, skidding to a stop in front of her desk.

Jimmy had been a mainstay of the *Planet* offices for a couple of years now, working his way up from copyboy to budding photojournalist. Right now he had a tall stack of old copies of the *Planet* in his arms, which he plunked down atop her bookcase with a deep sigh.

"Hi," she said, trying to work up a smile but ultimately failing. "What are you doing with those?"

"Sending them back to the morgue for Perry."

Perry White was the managing editor of the *Planet*. And he wasn't above giving Jimmy the most mundane tasks, despite his new position.

"He's working on some kind of statistical analysis," Jimmy told her. "He wants to know what kinds of headlines sell the most newspapers."

"That's nice," Lois said. She was so preoccupied with Clark, Jimmy's words were barely registering.

"Actually," said Jimmy, "he may be on to something. The other papers in town come up with some pretty snappy headlines. Ours are way too flat."

"Ours are dignified," Lois maintained.

Jimmy looked around. "Where's Clark? I bet he'll agree with me. Didn't you two go to that health fair together?"

"He had to go home," she lied. "*Newstime* had a booth, and Keith DeCann talked Clark into trying out their trampoline."

"I know how athletic he is," Jimmy said with a laugh. "Upset stomach?"

Lois nodded. "But not before he won a hundred bucks for his favorite charity."

"That's Clark." Jimmy picked up the stack of papers. "Still, it could've been much worse. Clark could've been bitten by that rabid dog." He shrugged. "Well, catch you later."

"I suppose," she said.

Lois didn't like not knowing where Clark was. Super though he might be, he could still get himself into trouble—and if she didn't know what had happened to him, how could she help get him out of it?

Superman was sitting quietly in the containment chamber at S.T.A.R. Labs, having long ago lost track of the time. It had been hours, it seemed, since he'd given Kitty Faulkner saliva samples so she could figure out what that spray had done to him.

He leapt to his feet when he heard a door open, and smiled.

It was Kitty, entering the room on the other side of the transparent wall. She was carrying a clipboard in one hand.

"I have news about the dog," she said, "and it isn't good."

Superman had seen it in her face even before she spoke. "Tell me," he said, his smile fading.

The doctor frowned. "It's dead. But not from the rabies—which it did indeed have. It's from . . . something else."

Superman swallowed. "And that is?"

She shook her head. "I don't know, exactly. It's a virus—I can tell you that much. But it's like no virus I've ever seen before. For one thing, it's extremely contagious, and extremely deadly. Second, it seems to be able to survive away from its host for long periods of time. That means if it gets airborne . . ."

Her voice trailed off meaningfully—but Superman got the picture anyway. A deadly airborne virus could be monstrous. If it got loose among the crowds in Metropolis, the resulting plague would make the Black Death look trivial by comparison.

"But that's not all of it," Kitty told him. "The virus is in *you* as well."

Superman felt a pit open in his stomach. He looked at the scientist. "What does that mean?"

She swallowed. "I think this thing was genetically engineered to invade the immune system—yours in particular. It's latched on to your cellular structure, and it's forcing your cells to make more of it."

"But how can that be?" he asked. "I'm invulnerable to parasites."

"As far as I can tell," she said, "the virus isn't going to affect you—at least, not in the sense that your cells will die, or that you'll show any symptoms. But you are a carrier, I'm afraid."

"A carrier . . ." Superman echoed numbly.

"That's right. More than likely, you're the one who infected the dog after you were exposed to the virus. He didn't have any of your resistances—and he only lasted a few hours. We can't allow anyone else to die—and if you go outside, that's what will happen." She took a deep breath and let it out. "For the time being," Kitty said, "you're going to have to remain in the containment chamber. I don't see any other answer."

"That's impossible," Superman argued, his hands balling into fists. He looked at them. "I've got a city to look after. People depend on me. I can't just—"

The scientist pounded on the transparent barrier, interrupting his protest. "Listen to me," she insisted. "If you leave, you'll do a lot more harm than good. You'll start a plague that might wipe out humanity. Superman . . . there's no cure for this disease. We can't let it go beyond these walls."

It was a bitter pill for him to swallow. He had always believed he'd been given his powers for a reason—to do good with them. But what good could even a Man of Steel do from inside this containment chamber?

He looked at Kitty again. "Is there any hope?" he asked softly.

"There's always hope," she told him. "We've just begun our work on this virus—just started identifying it. In a couple of weeks, we'll know whether any of the traditional drugs work on it. I have my doubts, but it's still a possibility. And then we'll start taking it apart one DNA strand at a time, looking for weaknesses."

Superman raised his chin defiantly. He'd come through a host of problems before. As bad as this one seemed, he'd have to trust Kitty to do her job and find a cure.

"It seems," he said slowly and reluctantly, "I have no choice in the matter. I guess I'm going to be your guest for a while."

Lois punched the phone number using the eraser end of her much-chewed pencil. "Come on, come on," she whispered as the phone on the other end began to ring.

On the third ring, Clark's answering machine picked up. After the beep, she said, "It's me. Let me know what's going on. I'm still at the *Planet*."

Hanging up, she began to chew her pencil again. What could have happened to him? It had been over two hours since Superman had appeared at the health fair. It wasn't like Clark to leave her wondering this long. Now she was really worried.

Suddenly Jimmy came rushing up to her desk, his eyes wide. "Quick, get to the chief's office," he said. "Something big's up with Superman."

"Superman?" Lois leapt to her feet.

She could feel her heart pounding, and a huge lump filled her throat. *Something's gone wrong,* she thought. *He's hurt or—*

Quickly she followed Jimmy into Perry's office. The editor's face looked ashen.

"Where's Clark?" he demanded. "I want him in on this, too."

"Sick," Lois said, providing the necessary cover. "I sent him to the doctor. What's up?"

"Listen to this," Perry told her. "Good thing I had my tape recorder handy. I started recording the call almost as soon as it started."

He hit the play button. The cassette player beeped, then a man's voice, sounding muffled and far away, began speaking.

". . . an important warning for the city of Metropolis. Superman has become the carrier of a highly contagious and deadly disease. He must be placed into quarantine immediately. If he goes near anyone else, if he touches anyone else, if he so much as breathes the same air as anyone else, he will be signing that person's death certificate. If Superman isn't already aware of this, he must be told—before it's too late. This is the only warning Metropolis will receive."

Then the caller hung up.

Lois's eyes rose to meet Perry's. She found her own shock and horror mirrored in his face. The news staggered her.

"The first thing he said," Perry went on, "is that this warning was going out simultaneously to every TV and radio station and newspaper in Metropolis. And then came the rest."

"I can't believe it," Lois said, feeling sick to her stomach. "I can't believe it."

"It's horrible, all right," Jimmy agreed. He had turned as white as the boss.

"I want you and Clark on this," Perry told Lois. "I don't care if you have to drag him out of open-heart surgery. Get me the exclusive. Get me Superman's story. Get me anything!"

"You've got it," she said, purely out of instinct.

Abruptly, as if that were a trigger, her brain clicked over into reporter mode. She'd always buried herself in her work in times of stress. This, she could already tell, was going to be one of those times.

Lois mulled the situation over. Who could be responsible for what had happened to Clark? Whose voice was on that tape?

She frowned, mentally running through a list of Superman's enemies. There were enough of them to fill a phone book, it seemed sometimes . . . but which of them might attack using a disease?

Lois began to understand why she hadn't heard from Clark. Apparently he'd quarantined himself somewhere. But where would he go?

Snapping her fingers, she came up with an answer. And then she bolted for the door.

CHAPTER FIVE

"This is a grim day for Metropolis," Perry White said to the *Planet*'s publisher, Franklin Stern, as they were coming back from a late lunch at a neighborhood delicatessen.

An hour earlier, he'd played the mysterious caller's tape for Lois and Jimmy. It had cut seriously into his appetite, though he hadn't seen fit to skip his weekly meeting with his old friend.

"You're not kidding," said Stern, an old-timer like Perry and just as tough in his own way. The man shook his head. "Crooks are going to hit this town like a ton of bricks. I'd take a vacation in the Bahamas till everything blows over, except I'm allergic to those godforsaken sunscreens."

"Have a little faith, Frank," Perry said. "We were able to rely on the police before we had Superman, after all. They'll just have to get the job done on their lonesome again."

The streetlight changed to red ahead of them, and they stopped at the corner. To their left, an armored bank truck stopped at the light, too.

Suddenly, before Perry's startled eyes, four shiny black limousines pulled up around the armored truck, surrounding it. The car doors flew open, and out poured a squad of twelve bandits, all wearing ski masks and brandishing Uzi submachine guns.

One of the bandits pumped two canisters of

knockout gas into the cab of the armored car. A thick, yellow-green gas poured out the vehicle's open windows, and the guard at the wheel slumped forward onto the horn, which blared loudly.

People began to turn and stare at the armored car. Perry grabbed his friend's arm and pointed.

"It's already beginning!" he said.

One of the bandits pointed his Uzi at the sky and fired half a round. People began to scream and dive for cover.

Stern pulled Perry down behind a FedEx drop-off box. Together they peeked out to watch. Stern began mumbling license plate numbers over and over to himself, trying, Perry guessed, to memorize them.

He shook his head. "Don't bother, Frank. Those cars will turn out to be stolen."

The other man grunted. "Probably—but if they don't, I've got 'em."

The bandits were placing charges of plastique around the back doors of the armored vehicle. Then they fled for the cover of their cars. A moment later, the explosive charges blew with a loud *crack*!

Though Perry had tried to cover his ears, they began to ring as the armored truck's doors slowly swung open. Quickly and methodically, the thieves loaded bags of money into the trunks of their limousines. Ten of them worked while two stood watch, their Uzis held at the ready.

In seconds, they had the armored vehicle cleaned out. They piled back into their cars and, as the red light changed to green, they accelerated smoothly, obeying the traffic laws.

Perry climbed to his feet and began dusting himself off. The yellow-green knockout gas had stopped pouring out of the cab, he noticed.

"I'll see if the driver needs any medical help," he said grimly, rolling up his sleeves. "You call the police."

"Right," Stern said, heading for a nearby pay phone.

Lois kept the radio in her car tuned to WLEX. As she was driving across the city, making her way through traffic, a special bulletin came on.

"Reports continue that Superman has been infected with a deadly new disease that some are already calling 'Virus X,'" the reporter said, "although no confirmation is available yet. We do know that criminal elements are loose across Metropolis in a rampage the likes of which has never been seen here before. We take you live to Jacob Brock at one of the crime scenes. Jake?"

"Right here, Harley," Jacob Brock said. His voice was muffled by traffic noises and the sounds of approaching sirens. "I'm on Fifth Avenue, where an armored car was just robbed. With me is Police Commissioner William Henderson."

Lois knew the man well. She turned up the radio's volume.

"Apparently," said Henderson, "the armored vehicle was stopped at a red light when four cars pulled up." Quickly, he ran through the events as he understood them. "It seems every petty thief in the city is out," the commissioner concluded. "Tell your listeners to stay home and bolt the doors until the police and Superman get things back under control."

"What about the virus Superman has allegedly contracted?" Brock asked him.

"For all I know," Henderson said, "it's some kind of practical joke. I'm sure Superman will show up soon to set things right—and then you'll see how fast these punks end up behind bars!"

"There you have it," Jacob said, "straight from the mouth of Police Commissioner William Henderson. Back to you, Harley."

"Thanks, Jake," Harley's voice said. "Turning to sports—"

Lois shut the radio off. She had to think.

It chilled her to think that crooks had got away with such a blatant, in-your-face crime in Metropolis. Yet that's just what they had done— and Superman was evidently powerless to stop them.

What's more, things could only get worse. Stepping harder on the gas pedal, she wove through traffic, more eager than ever to reach her destination.

*   *   *

Twenty minutes later, Lois pulled up to the entrance of S.T.A.R. Labs. S.T.A.R. was a non-profit institution on the cutting edge of scientific and technical research.

Superman had worked with the scientists there before. He knew how advanced some of their facilities were. If he really were infected with a disease, S.T.A.R. Labs would probably have been the first place he turned to.

Everything looked normal enough here, she thought uneasily. The gates were wide open; business seemed to be continuing as usual.

Had she guessed wrong? Had Superman gone somewhere else in his moment of need?

A bored-looking guard stepped out of the little guardhouse next to the gates and strolled over, clipboard in hand. Rolling down her window, Lois put on her most charming smile.

The guard, though, drew up short, frowning. "I know you," he said. "You're Lois Lane, that reporter from the *Daily Planet*. I see your picture in the paper. You wrote that election fraud story last week."

"That's right," she said, still smiling with effort. "It's nice to meet a fan of my work."

The guard smiled. "I may be a fan, Ms. Lane, but I'm afraid I can't let anyone in without an appointment, and you're not on my list for today." He waved his clipboard as if that made all the difference. "If you want, I can give you our publicity director's phone number. Maybe he can set you up for a tour next week."

"Actually, I'm here to see Superman," she said.

"Uh . . . Superman?" the guard stammered, obviously taken by surprise. The expression on his face gave the whole story away.

I was right! Lois thought triumphantly. She hadn't become an ace reporter on looks alone. Instinct and a nose for trouble helped, and she had both.

The guard fumbled for words, realizing he might have given Superman's presence here away. "I, uh—I gotta check. Don't think we have anyone here by that, uh, name today, though."

"So he was here yesterday, but you released him?" Lois asked sweetly. "Is that what you're saying?"

The guard frowned, unwilling to say anything that would get him in any more trouble. "Let me check for you," he muttered. By then a blush had begun to spread up his neck and cheeks. "Gotta call the boss."

I can't let him stop me, Lois thought. The guard's boss would only stall her or put her off. Good reporters needed not only great instincts and a nose for trouble, but steel nerves.

Perhaps that's why Clark's so good, she added inwardly. Whose nerves would be steelier than the Man of Steel's?

As the guard entered his little station next to

the gate, the reporter saw her chance. It was now or never.

Clenching her teeth, she floored the accelerator and raced past him—through the open gate and into S.T.A.R. Labs' main compound. In the rearview mirror she could see the guard shouting frantically into his walkie-talkie.

As she drove, Lois saw a long, enclosed plastic walkway attached to an entrance into one of the buildings. She didn't know what it was for, exactly, but it didn't look like a good sign.

Pulling up in front of that building's main doors, she got out and glanced back toward the guardhouse. The guard had closed both front gates and was running toward her as fast as he could.

At this distance, it wouldn't take him more than twenty or thirty seconds to catch up with her. She'd have to make the best of her head start.

Darting through the building's front door, she came face-to-face with a startled-looking man in a white lab coat. He had a tray of sealed vials in his hands.

"Who are you?" he demanded. "What are you doing here?"

"I have to see Superman," she said. She leaned forward to read his name tag. "Which way is he, Mr. MacClennan?"

"I'm afraid he's not here," MacClennan began. He peered over her shoulder; Lois knew he could see the guard approaching across the parking lot. "And I don't think you should be either."

Ignoring the comment, she stuck out her hand. "Lois Lane from the *Daily Planet*."

He shifted the tray of vials to one side and shook her hand. "Pleased to meet you, Ms. Lane," he said. "Really, though, if Superman were here, I'd know it."

"Look," Lois said, "if you won't let me see Superman, at least let me see Dr. Kitty Faulkner. I know her presence here isn't classified. Please—it's very important. Superman will want to see me. I have important news for him."

"I think Dr. Faulkner is somewhere in the building," MacClennan said slowly, still gazing over her shoulder.

Just then the guard, panting heavily, burst through the doors.

"Ms. Lane—" the guard gasped. "If I were you, I'd leave . . . right this second. Otherwise . . . I'll have you arrested . . . for trespassing!"

He tried to take her arm, but Lois moved away, beyond his grasp.

"Please," she appealed, "you don't understand. I really need to speak with Dr. Faulkner. Believe me, I wouldn't be making such a fuss if it weren't important."

MacClennan sighed. "Keep her here, Bob," he said to the guard. "I'll find the doctor." He turned and hurried up the corridor, through a set of double doors, and vanished from sight.

Lois waited impatiently. A minute later, MacClennan returned with Kitty Faulkner on his heels. She wore a white lab coat much like his and had a pair of rubber gloves, which she slowly peeled off. She didn't shake the hand Lois held out.

"Ms. Lane," the scientist said with a sigh, "I'm afraid you've been given some wrong information. We're very busy here. If you'll accompany Bob off the premises . . ."

"Look," Lois replied, refusing to back down, "time is important here, so let's cut to the chase. I know Superman's here," she bluffed. "I have two witnesses in a helicopter who saw you take him in through that tube thing outside."

Kitty exchanged a guilty glance with MacClennan but didn't reply.

"Listen," Lois went on, "everyone knows about the virus. All the radio and TV stations are carrying the story. And it makes sense that Superman would come to you with it. You're the only place around here equipped to deal with something like that." She paused. "I apologize for barging in like this, but I have news that's for Superman's ears only. He'll want to see me. If someone will just ask him, he'll confirm that."

The scientist looked at Lois for a long moment. Her expression didn't give anything away.

"I'm still not admitting anything," Kitty said at last, "but I'll be right back." Then she turned and strode off the way she'd come.

The guard continued to glare at Lois. MacClennan looked distinctly uncomfortable; he began to fidget with the tubes on his tray, rearranging them, then putting them back the way they'd been.

Lois took a deep breath, then began to pace uneasily. What was taking Kitty Faulkner so long? And what, exactly, was going on behind those double doors? What had they done to Superman—to Clark? she wondered.

The breath caught in her throat when Kitty finally returned a few minutes later. She turned first to Bob the guard.

"I'll take care of Ms. Lane. You can return to your post," she told him. "Open the gates and make sure everything looks normal again."

Nodding, he complied. As he left, he could be heard muttering to himself—something about pushy reporters. Lois couldn't help smiling a little.

Then she looked at the scientist. "So?" Lois prodded gently.

Kitty frowned. "Look," she said, "I'll help you, Lois. But you have to agree not to publish anything about his being here. I want your word on that. You and Superman are close friends, but I generally don't trust reporters farther than I can throw them. If we're going to be of any help to him, we can't have a mob of TV reporters storming our front gates. That would only help whoever did this to track Superman here."

"Agreed," Lois said with a sigh of relief. That was a condition she could live with. "Believe me, I want to help Superman as much as you do. Right now, that's more important to me than any news story."

"All right, then," said Kitty. "Follow me." She turned and led the way deeper into the facility.

They didn't have to go far. Lois turned a corner and suddenly there he was—Superman. But a very un-super-looking Superman, dressed now in a pale blue gown instead of his usual red and blue costume, standing impatiently before a glass wall. For the first time since she'd met him, he seemed as vulnerable as any other being.

Instantly aware of her presence, he looked up. The expression on his face spoke volumes about how he felt being separated from the world— being separated from *her*.

"Hello, Ms. Lane," Superman said through an elaborate intercom. He forced a smile. "I'm afraid my costume is at the cleaners."

Lois turned to Kitty. "Can I have a minute alone to talk to him?" she asked.

The scientist frowned but gave a curt nod. "I'll be over here," she said. She crossed to the far side of the room.

Lois turned to Superman, and the words caught in her throat. There were a thousand things she'd wanted to say to him, and suddenly she couldn't think of any of them.

She felt a cold lump form in her stomach, and tears came unbidden to her eyes. If only she were truly alone with him. If only she could tell him how she really felt. But now, here, with the S.T.A.R. Labs people looking on, that was impossible.

"Superman," she moaned, unconsciously pressing her fingertips against the glass barrier. "I'm sorry. I'm so sorry."

His eyes echoed her emotion. But his voice was clear and steady. "How is it out there?" he asked her.

Dutifully, she told him about the armored car heist that Perry had witnessed. "They did it in broad daylight," she said. "I still can't believe their nerve."

"Then it's begun," Superman said quietly. He looked as if he were enduring a physical pain. "I knew something like this was going to happen, but I didn't think it would start so quickly." He made a fist, then released it slowly.

Lois could only imagine the frustration he was feeling—the inner turmoil. "Is there anything I can do?" she asked.

Slowly, even a little sadly, Superman shook his head. "No, Ms. Lane. But thanks for telling me the truth—no matter how much it pains me to hear it."

Lois felt so helpless—almost as if she were on the wrong side of the barrier herself. As long as

Superman was penned up in there, a part of her was imprisoned as well.

"Is there anything you need? Anything I can bring you?" she pressed.

"I can't think of anything," he answered softly. "They're taking good care of me here. If anyone can find a cure, Dr. Faulkner can." Abruptly, his expression changed—became more determined. "No," he said, "I take that back. I *can* think of something. Use your contacts. See if you can find out who's behind all this."

Lois stepped back. She was having trouble swallowing; she thought she might burst into tears at any moment, and she didn't want Superman to see her that way. But it tore her up inside to see him here, caged like an animal in a zoo.

"I'll do what I can," she whispered. "And . . . I'll speak to those out-of-towners you introduced me to," meaning his parents.

The Man of Steel swallowed. "Of course. I'd appreciate that."

He reached out as if to touch her, and for an instant their hands rested on the glass together, barely a quarter of an inch apart. But it might as well have been a thousand miles, for all the good it did them.

Then, reluctantly, Lois had to take her hand back. She wanted to stay there, but she had to be strong. Strong for Clark. She had to do something.

Lois took a breath and let it out. "I'll call back when I have something to tell you," she said more loudly, for the benefit of Kitty Faulkner. "Will that be okay, Superman?"

"Anytime," he replied, trying to make a joke of it. "I'm not going anywhere."

Biting her lip, Lois turned away. Dr. Faulkner was waiting by the door for her. Together they headed back toward the building's exit.

"I'll make sure your name is on the guard's list of people to admit," the scientist told her. "I'm sorry I doubted you, Ms. Lane, but I'm sure you understand. I couldn't take any chances."

"Sure," Lois said absently. "I understand."

They reached the doors to the outside, and Kitty swung one open for her. Lois went out into the bright sunshine, blinked a few times at the tears that still filled her eyes, then climbed into her car and started the engine.

For a while she just sat there. She had a lot to think about suddenly . . . and none of it was good.

What if Clark had to stay in that place for the rest of his life? What if she never got a chance to embrace him again—to feel his strong arms fold around her?

No, she told herself. That kind of thinking wouldn't get her anywhere. If she was going to be of any help, she had to adopt a positive outlook.

Superman was going to beat this thing. She was going to make sure of that.

But where to start? Who would know about strange and obscure viruses? Still thinking, she put her car in gear and headed for the highway.

In Smallville, Martha Kent clutched her telephone receiver so hard her knuckles turned white. The phone on the other end began to ring.

"Come on," she whispered to herself. "Pick up, please pick up!"

The phone rang once. Twice. Three times . . . and then came an all-too-familiar click. Lois Lane's voice said, "Hi, I'm not here right now. Here's the beep. You know what to do."

Martha didn't wait for the beep. She just sighed and hung up. She'd already left three messages for Lois that afternoon, and one more wouldn't do a bit of good.

"Well?" Jonathan said from behind her.

She looked at him. His face was drawn with worry—just as hers must have been.

"She's not back yet," Martha told him, and she heard the huskiness in her voice that came from holding back tears.

Jonathan moved toward her and gave her a hug. She drew strength from his quiet, stoic presence.

They'd been watching CNN all afternoon, waiting for more news on their son. There hadn't been anything except the one story, repeated over and over, that he had been infected with a virus that was potentially lethal for anyone who came in contact with him.

Suddenly the phone rang. Martha clutched at it. "Hello?" she said in a trembling voice.

"Martha? It's Lois."

The older woman tensed up inside. "Lois, what is it? Have you seen Clark? Is he as bad off as people say?"

Lois told her what she knew. By the end of the conversation, Martha was both more alarmed and more relieved. But at least she wasn't dealing with rumors and hearsay anymore. She knew the truth.

"What is it?" asked Jonathan, more anxious than she had seen him in a long time. "What's she saying?"

Martha passed on the information Lois had given her. She saw her husband turn pale and look for a chair. When he found one, he sat down heavily.

"Clark . . ." he sighed.

"He'll be all right," Lois assured Martha. "I know he will. Clark's strong, thanks to you and Jonathan. Somehow he'll come through."

Martha nodded, though of course Lois couldn't see her. "I know he will, dear. He always has." She paused. "But what about you? Are *you* going to be okay?"

"Don't worry about me," said Lois. "As long as I've got something to do, I'll be fine. And right now, I'm putting all my energy into finding out who did this. Once we know that, maybe we can find a cure."

"Just be careful," Martha told her. "That someone may be dangerous."

"I'll be careful," the younger woman said. "I promise. 'Bye."

"Good-bye," Martha replied.

As she hung up the phone, she exchanged glances with Jonathan again. It looked like it was going to be a very long night.

CHAPTER SIX

As Superman watched Lois leave, he felt more alone than ever. And more helpless, as well. He was used to being the master of his own fate. But in this instance, his fate lay in the hands of Kitty Faulkner and her team of scientists.

The Man of Steel crossed to his chair and sat, burying his face in his hands. He'd been through a lot since his arrival in Metropolis, when he first put his powers to public use.

He could fight a hundred men, even a thousand, and come out on top. But now he'd been stopped by something a human couldn't even see without the aid of a microscope.

Without meaning to, he flashed back on the moment when, as a child in Smallville, he first realized the extent of his powers. A ball had rolled under his father's pickup truck, and in his eagerness to get it, he picked up the back end of the truck.

He hadn't thought about it. He had just done it. It was only after he heard his mother's startled cry that he realized the magnitude of his feat and let the pickup come crashing to the ground.

One evening, after dinner, his parents sat him down on the front porch. With the sun setting over the fields, they stressed how important it was for him to keep his amazing strength a secret.

After all, they said, there were people who

might become afraid of him if they knew the truth. There were those who might think of him as some kind of monster, and still others who might try to exploit him for their own gain.

At the time, he hadn't understood all of what his parents were saying. But he understood enough to know that he had to keep his strength to himself.

And later, in his teens, when his other powers kicked in—when he learned to see great distances and to fly—he continued to heed his parents' warning. The more different he became, the less he wanted to be thought of that way. He didn't want to be shunned or distrusted—just to be treated as a normal young man.

Now, someone had made of him just what he'd feared. He'd been turned into a pariah—apparently just to keep him out of the way while Metropolis was robbed and ravaged.

Superman's fingers curled into fists. No, he thought. He wouldn't let it happen. Somehow, some way, he had to prove he could beat this. Even with the virus, there had to be a way for him to protect his city.

Suddenly the metal box in the wall to his right opened, revealing a tray of food and a pitcher of water. He took them from the box and closed it again, then brought the food and water to the folding table he had been given.

The Man of Steel noted the presence of someone in a containment suit on the other side of the transparent barrier. It was MacClennan, Kitty's assistant. Apparently MacClennan was the one who had just provided Superman with his meal.

He waved to the scientist. "Thanks," he said, speaking loudly enough to be heard through the barrier, "though I really don't much feel like eating."

"You need to keep up your strength," the scientist replied through his faceplate. His voice sounded muffled. "In case the virus begins to affect you, I mean."

Heeding MacClennan's advice, Superman removed the tray's plastic cover, revealing two hamburgers, several packets of ketchup, a can of Soder Cola, and a straw. Not exactly a meal fit for a king, he reflected, but he'd had a lot worse.

"Sorry," said the scientist, "but that's the best we could do on short notice."

"No problem," Superman assured him. "It's fine."

He peeled back the paper wrapper protecting the hamburger, applied some ketchup, and took a bite. On the other side of the barrier, MacClennan brought his thumb and forefinger together and gave his charge the okay sign.

Of course, the gesture was a bit awkward, given the bulkiness of his containment suit. But then, beggars couldn't be choosers. At least the man was kept apart from the virus.

Kept apart . . . ?

Suddenly Superman put his hamburger down.

"What's wrong?" asked MacClennan, obviously concerned.

"Nothing," said the Man of Steel. He smiled. "I just had an idea."

CHAPTER SEVEN

Professor Killgrave came a few minutes late to his meeting with Smith, which was again held in the operating theater. This way, he thought, I will look like the most important man there. They will have to wait for me.

But when he strolled through the doors into the room, hands in his pockets to effect a casual demeanor, he found the place empty. Even the observation gallery was deserted.

A cold anger swept through him. How dare Smith stand him up? Smith's people had arranged for this meeting, not him. Didn't they realize how valuable his time was?

As if on cue, the doors swung open again, and Smith strolled in, followed by his bodyguards. He looked as if he didn't have a care in the world—the very picture of a high-powered executive on his way to a leisurely lunch.

"What kept you?" Killgrave demanded a little shrilly.

"Business," Smith said idly.

He gestured, and the bodyguard to his left slapped the handle of a small briefcase into his palm. Smith slowly set the briefcase down flat on the table where the two mice had been, flipped the twin locks, and opened the lid.

The briefcase was packed with hundred-dollar bills. A lot of them.

Killgrave nodded. "My cut?" he asked, though it wasn't really a question.

"Your cut," Smith agreed. "A quarter of a million dollars."

"That's all?" Killgrave asked, frowning a bit. He had expected more. A lot more.

But judging by the scowl spreading across Smith's face, it would have been foolish to press his point. With the man's henchmen around, Killgrave was clearly outmatched.

But that wouldn't always be the case.

"This is only the beginning," Smith said, almost as if he were talking to himself. "We'll pull a job a day from now on . . . till Metropolis is sucked dry as an old bone."

Killgrave began to smile. That sounded a lot better, he thought. A quarter of a million dollars a day would do quite nicely—for the present, at least.

"I'll be back tomorrow," Smith went on. "I still have a few more arrangements to make for tomorrow's heist."

"What's the job?" the scientist asked.

Smith only shook his head. "My plans are on a need-to-know basis."

Killgrave shrugged. "As you wish."

The scientist began pulling out rubber-banded stacks of hundred-dollar bills from the briefcase and piling them up on the table. Halfway through the process, he made a show of accidentally dropping a stack on the floor.

Everyone's eyes were drawn in the direction of the fallen money. That's when Killgrave took advantage of the opportunity to slip a couple of small devices into one of the briefcase's pockets.

"Oops," he said, bending and retrieving the packet of money. "Don't want that to get away." Then he returned to emptying the briefcase.

A couple of Smith's thugs exchanged glances, silently commenting on Killgrave's clumsiness. One of them snorted, clearly amused.

Let them laugh, thought the scientist, as he pulled out the last of the money and returned the briefcase to a henchman. *The last laugh will be mine.*

As Lois walked up the stairs to Professor Emil Hamilton's lab, she reflected on how much time had passed since she had seen the professor last. Months, at least. But she had no doubt that he would be glad to see her.

Hamilton knew she was Superman's friend. And at a time like this, Superman's friends had to stick together.

Arriving at the apartment, she knocked on the first door to her right. For a moment there was silence. Then the door opened, and a bearded, middle-aged man peered through the space between the door and the jamb.

"Lois?" said Hamilton. "Lois Lane?" He opened the door wide for her, his expression brightening. "Please come in."

She entered the room, which was really the professor's living space. His experiments were conducted in the several rooms behind it, which had been converted into lab enclosures.

Hamilton absently tucked his shirt into his pants and indicated a couch with a gesture. "Have a seat, Lois. I believe I know why you're here. It's about Superman, isn't it?"

That much was obvious. She had come here in the hope that Hamilton, perhaps the only man ever to have had a chance to examine Superman at length, might be able to shed some light on the virus.

Emil Hamilton owed Superman a great deal. After all, it was the Man of Steel who had helped the professor over some rough spots and enabled him to obtain financing for his work. But as many times as he had paid Superman back for his kindness, he was always eager to do more.

"I suppose you've heard what happened to him," Lois began.

Hamilton frowned. "There was something about it on the radio, but it seemed so ridiculous that, frankly, I didn't believe it."

"Ridiculous?" Lois asked. "Why?"

The professor shrugged. "No terrestrial disease could possibly affect Superman the way they said. Do you know what a virus is, exactly, Ms. Lane?"

"Some kind of germ?"

"Not at all," he told her. "A virus is a strand of DNA that insinuates itself into a cell and programs it to create more strands of virus-DNA, which in turn invade other cells. Unfortunately, the cells so used are destroyed. It's this destruction that provokes the body's natural defenses, causing the symptoms of coughing, fever, dizziness, nausea, and so on."

Lois nodded. "And you're saying Superman should be immune to all this?"

"Exactly," said Hamilton. "There's no DNA on Earth strong enough to reprogram a Kryptonian cell. That's why Superman is the picture of health. Every single cell in his body is absolutely, one hundred percent perfect. No illness, no disease, no infections."

"But the virus *is* there," Lois reminded him. "In his body, I mean. I've met the people who are working with him to try to find a cure. They're taking this matter quite seriously."

The professor absorbed the information, then began to pace. It was clear that he was giving this all the brainpower he could muster. Finally he stopped pacing and looked at her.

"There is one other possibility," he said. "What if this virus—or at least its basic material— originated somewhere other than on Earth?"

Lois thought about it. "You mean it could be a Kryptonian virus?"

"It's possible," he conceded. "Superman made it to Earth. So did kryptonite. Why not a Kryptonian virus? It might even have been carried to Earth with Superman."

The reporter shook her head. "That doesn't sound very likely."

"It's not," Hamilton admitted. "But is it any more unlikely than Superman himself? He defies every likelihood."

"Point taken," Lois said. "Are there any other possibilities?"

Hamilton stroked his beard. "Not really. Oh, I suppose the virus could be a mutation that has, somehow, found a weakness in Superman's body chemistry. But the odds have to be trillions to one against it. If I had to guess, I'd say it came from Krypton or some other planet."

Lois sighed. "And a cure?"

Hamilton spread his hands helplessly. "I assume he's at S.T.A.R. Labs. That's where I'd go if I were him. If that's what he's done, he's in the best hands possible."

"I hope you're right," Lois said.

The professor smiled sadly. "I wish I could be of more help," he told her.

"That's all right," Lois assured him. "You've been plenty helpful." He'd given her a lot to think about, in fact. "I guess I ought to be going now."

Hamilton showed her to the door and made her promise to call again if she needed anything. Then Lois descended the stairs and hurried back out to her car.

The alien-origin angle was one she hadn't thought of. Perhaps the people at S.T.A.R. Labs hadn't thought of it yet, either.

She used her car phone to call Kitty Faulkner. It took ten minutes for her to get through a maze of receptionists and staff bureaucrats, but at last Kitty came to the phone.

"I'm sorry, Ms. Lane, but what is it?" she asked. "I'm in the middle of some very important tests on our . . . um, guest."

Quickly Lois told her about Professor Hamilton's theories.

"It hadn't occurred to me that it might be an alien virus," Kitty said slowly, "because we recognized parts of it early on—parts taken from influenza, Ebola, and a few other terrestrial viruses. But there *is* one part we can't seem to figure out. If it's something alien, then everything suddenly makes a lot more sense." She paused. "Thank you, Ms. Lane. You may have been more help than you realize."

Lois smiled, feeling a little better about having called. The scientist certainly sounded a lot warmer now. "If I find out anything else," she said, "I'll let you know."

"Please do," Kitty said and hung up.

Lois paused thoughtfully, the receiver in her hand. At least she'd accomplished something.

Progress—any progress, no matter how slight—had to be taken as an encouraging sign. Somehow, she resolved, she was going to help get Superman out of his predicament, no matter how long it took. After all, she couldn't bear the thought of never being able to hold Clark in her arms again.

Her next move was pretty clear, at least in her own mind. She had to work on the alien-virus angle, she told herself, leaning back into her car seat.

First, Lois thought, *for the sake of argument, let's say this virus only recently came to Earth.* That made sense to her. After all, Superman had been around for a while, and no one had sprung it on him until now.

Second, someone must have found this virus once it came to Earth. That meant there might be a record of it. But who would have access to that kind of information?

She thought for a moment, and then an answer came to her. It was a good thing she had such a sharp memory.

The Kodiak Institute of Extraterrestrial Research. She'd seen them quoted any number of times on stories that came in over the Associated Press news feeds. They were in New England somewhere, weren't they?

She hesitated a second, then dialed the *Daily Planet.*

A moment later she heard a voice. "Hello, Olsen here."

"This is Lois," she said. "I need your help."

She knew he'd be more than happy to lend a hand. "Sure, Lois. You name it."

"First," she told him, "I need you to look up

73

a group called the Kodiak Institute of Extraterrestrial Research. I want to know where they are and who's in charge."

"Uh, okay. That's going to be in the computer somewhere, isn't it?"

It was a rhetorical question. Jimmy knew his way around computers about as well as anyone. Lois heard him typing on a keyboard. A moment later, he gave a small grunt of triumph.

"Indian Path, Maine," he announced. He gave her the phone number, which she quickly took down. "Emmett Plymouth is listed as the director."

"Great, Jimmy. Thanks."

"What was the second thing?" he asked.

"I need you to leave a message for Perry," Lois told him. "Let him know that Clark and I are going to be in the field for the next few days, tracking down more information about Superman and his condition. We'll have a scoop before we're done."

"How is Superman?" Jimmy asked. "Have you heard anything?"

Lois sighed. "He's been better, Jimmy. But for now, that's all I can say. I've been sworn to secrecy."

He sounded disappointed. "Okay—I guess. Say . . . you wouldn't happen to need a photographer up there in Maine?" he asked hopefully. "I'd be happy to drop everything and join you—"

"No," Lois said firmly. She couldn't let Jimmy

see that Clark wasn't with her. That meant she had to lie to him, as much as she regretted it. "Sorry, but the people we're talking to want to keep their names off the record. You wouldn't have much to do up here."

Lois felt bad about keeping Jimmy in the dark and decided a little tidbit wouldn't hurt.

"Listen," she told him, "I do have one lead— if you can keep it under your hat."

"You got it," Jimmy promised.

"Okay, then. This virus Superman is suffering from? It may be of alien origin."

Her friend whistled. "Alien . . . as in not of this Earth?"

"That's right," Lois confirmed.

"Wow! That's why you're headed for Indian Path, right?"

"Right. Now take care, and we'll see you soon. And don't get yourself hurt covering that crime spree."

"I'll do my best," Jimmy replied.

Lois hung up and replaced the phone in its cradle. Then, pulling out her road atlas, she flipped to Maine and began searching for Indian Path.

It took her a while to find the place. But she finally put her finger on it. As luck would have it, it was at the top of the page, near the Canadian border.

Starting her car, Lois took a deep breath. She had one heck of a long drive ahead of her.

CHAPTER EIGHT

Jimmy Olsen rolled out of bed at 6:00 A.M. sharp, morning light streaming in through his window. His eyes were bleary; he wished he could have slept another two hours.

But Tammy Benson, his latest girlfriend, was due at the airport, and he planned to be there to greet her. She'd been working a lot of overseas trips in her job as a stewardess with LexAir, and he hadn't seen her in a couple of weeks. Besides, with the crime wave going on, he wanted to make sure she got in safely.

Jimmy showered, shaved, splashed on a little cologne, and put on some of the clothes Tammy had helped him pick out for his birthday months earlier. Then, grabbing his camera, he headed for the subway.

Tammy sometimes complained that he lugged his photographic equipment everywhere they went. But as he'd explained, he never knew when a story would pop up. He'd got more than his share of prize-winning scoops that way.

The trip to the airport was uneventful. He kept the camera bag on his lap, dozing through half-closed eyes.

At last he reached the airport. He took the escalator up to the terminal level and scanned the arrival flight monitor. Tammy's plane was running a typical half hour late. He headed for the gate.

Unfortunately security seemed to have been tightened. The guards stopped him at the metal detector.

"Ticket?" a female guard asked.

"I'm meeting one of the flight attendants," he said. "I haven't seen her in two weeks, and—"

"No tickets?" she asked again.

"No."

"What's in the bag?"

"This?" Jimmy hefted his camera bag. "My equipment. I'm a photographer for the *Daily Planet*."

"Got some identification?"

Jimmy fished around for his wallet and pulled out his staff photo ID card. "Here."

The woman took the card, eyed the photo, then looked at him carefully. "This doesn't look like you," she said.

"It's a bad photo," Jimmy replied.

The guard frowned. "And you have no ticket?" she asked.

"No," he confirmed.

"Then I can't let you in. It would cost me my job."

Jimmy sighed. It looked as if he would have to meet Tammy here by security with the rest of the crowd. He couldn't wait for things to get back to normal.

Perry White arrived an hour early at the *Daily Planet*. He wanted to get a head start on reviewing the stories filed the night before. With Superman out of the picture, there was certainly no shortage of news to pick from.

As he entered his office, he noticed the message light on his answering machine blinking steadily. When he punched the button, it told him that seventeen people had called.

Sighing, Perry put down the bag he'd picked up at the coffee shop downstairs and took off his coat. Then he extracted his coffee and jelly doughnut, took a sip of the former and a bite of the latter, and began listening to his messages.

Nothing that can't wait until nine o'clock, he thought, as he neared the end of the list. The last message was from Jimmy Olsen.

It said, "I left a note from Lois and Clark for you. It's under your coffee. Catch you later, Chief."

Perry lifted his coffee cup. Sure enough, on the pad underneath was a message in Jimmy's untidy scrawl.

Mr. White—
Lois called late last night. She's on the Superman story with Clark and says they won't be in the office for a few days. Apparently they're on to something BIG.
—Jimmy O.

Perry stared at the paper for a minute, then crumpled it up and tossed it into the trash can. Of course Lois hadn't left a number where she could be reached. Typical.

If she and Clark weren't his best reporters, he might have suspected they were taking a vacation together in the Bahamas. But no, he knew them better than that. They'd be back, and with the story of the week.

Perry took another sip of his coffee, switched on his computer monitor, and got to work. With all the crime stories he had to consider, the whereabouts of Lois and Clark soon became the farthest thing from his mind.

Still stuck in the waiting area outside the metal detector, Jimmy peered out the huge plate glass window overlooking the landing field. LexAir Flight 444 from Mexico City, with Tammy aboard, was taxiing across the tarmac in the direction of the nearest gate.

He could tell it was Flight 444 by the arrivals board, which listed it as due to arrive right about now. No other LexAir flights were due to land in this part of the airport for another half hour.

Minutes later a swarm of people emerged from the gate and streamed down the corridor toward the security checkpoint. They were speaking in worried tones in English, Spanish, and a few other languages—lots of tourists coming to Metropolis from foreign countries, lots of businessmen, but all seemingly concerned about the Metropolis crime wave.

Tammy would be off the plane last, along with the rest of the crew. Idly Jimmy watched the baggage handlers down below as they opened the doors to the cargo hold in the plane's belly.

They unloaded a few suitcases, then began pulling out a series of wooden packing crates. Jimmy wondered what they were but couldn't make out the stamps on the boxes. Maybe Tammy could clue him in.

As he was watching, a food service van drove up to the plane to restock it for its next flight. From what Tammy had told him, the airline's food had improved immensely after it had contracted with a new company for its prepared meals.

Jimmy was hungry. He had missed breakfast in his rush to get to the airport. He was trying to imagine what kinds of meals might be in the van when its doors opened and a couple of uniformed men got out.

Jimmy's eyes opened wide. The men were wearing ski masks and cradling automatic weapons. They were gesturing to the baggage handlers to back off.

He gasped. It was a holdup of some kind—going on right below him!

"Security!" Jimmy yelled, drawing the attention of the checkpoint guards. "There are men down there with guns!" He pointed to the plane.

Instantly one of the guards activated a walkie-talkie and began to report the terrorists, while two more opened a special security door and

Perry White (Lane Smith), Jimmy Olsen (Justin Whalin), Lois Lane (Teri Hatcher),
Clark Kent (Dean Cain), Martha Kent (K Callan) and Jonathan Kent (Eddie Jones)

Lois Lane and Superman

Clark Kent and Lois Lane

Superman

Lois and Superman

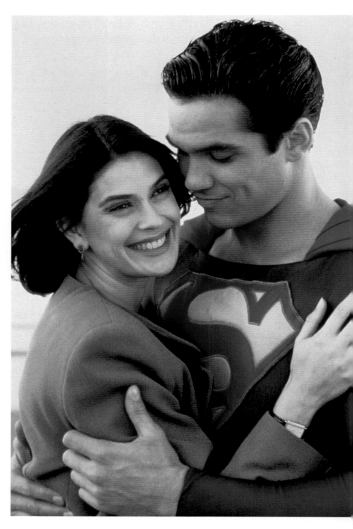

Lois and Superman

Superman

Superman and Lois Lane

raced down a set of stairs. Jimmy hesitated for a moment as he considered the open door, caught between his desire to obey the law and his instincts as a journalist.

His instincts won. Removing the lens cover from his camera, he tore down the stairs after the guards. Fortunately he had loaded a new roll of film the night before.

No sooner had he reached the tarmac than he began snapping photos. The guards were too busy racing toward the scene of the crime to notice him.

Jimmy watched, ignoring his fear in order to capture the incident for the *Planet*. The men who'd emerged from the food service van began firing at the guards. The guards fired back.

In the end, however, the crooks and their weapons proved more effective. Both guards were wounded, one in the arm and the other in the leg.

Seeing what had happened to the guards, the baggage handlers thrust their hands into the air. At an order from the robbers, they began loading the wooden crates into the van.

Jimmy finished his roll of film, switched on the rapid rewinder, and waited impatiently while the camera did its work. At last he popped in a new roll.

There was nothing he could do to stop the heist. But if he did his job, there would be a record of the crime, maybe even a way of identifying those responsible.

He glanced around, hoping for the arrival of the police. But he didn't see any. He had a sinking feeling that by the time they arrived, it would be too late.

If only Superman were still in action. He would have made short work of these creeps by now. But of course, that wasn't going to happen—not if the Man of Steel was really afflicted with some terrible virus.

The packing crates were all aboard the van now. Their work done, the two men in the ski masks leapt back into their vehicle and closed the doors behind them. An accomplice at the wheel began to drive off.

Suddenly a blur appeared in the sky, glinting with sunlight. Jimmy's heart skipped a beat. Could it be…?

He raised his camera, adjusted the telephoto lens, and began snapping shots. Just in case.

The figure landed before the van, one hand outstretched as if to stop it. But it wasn't Superman—or was it?

The figure wore a strange, bulky outfit, almost like a space suit. Who could it be? Jimmy thought.

He kept snapping shots as the van crashed into the figure at full speed—and the front end of the vehicle crumpled as if it were made of tinfoil.

Jimmy grinned. No doubt about it. It really *was* Superman!

CHAPTER NINE

The van's tyres spun and squealed, but to no avail. Superman held it in place with one hand.

Behind the transparent faceplate of the special containment suit Kitty had designed at his request, the Man of Tomorrow smiled. Things were certainly looking up.

He could again guard his city from thieves and thugs, albeit from inside a hazardous-environment suit. Never mind that *he* was the hazard.

They still had a few bugs in the system to work out, of course. He glanced at the digital readout just inside the faceplate, which indicated that he'd expended the last of his air supply almost fifty minutes ago.

Thanks to his powerful lungs, however, he'd been able to double the time afforded him by the oxygen in his built-in tanks. He had put the extra time to good use, continuing to address a wave of petty crime all across Metropolis.

Luckily he'd swung out over the airport before heading back to S.T.A.R. Labs. Otherwise he would have missed this heist.

As the two armed bandits in the back of the van opened the door and leapt out, raising their weapons to fire, Superman stepped forward and crushed the weapons' barrels. His only fear at that moment was that he might tear his containment suit. A bullet or a piece of flying shrapnel would do the trick, and a hole in the containment suit would almost certainly release the virus.

As the two criminals tried to escape on foot, Superman chased them down with superspeed, grabbed them by their collars, and dragged them back. By that time, their accomplice in the front of the vehicle was trying to get away as well.

Still burdened with the other crooks, the Man of Steel positioned himself in the third robber's path and knocked him off his feet. And by the time he got up, the police were arriving in half a dozen patrol cars.

Turning the trio over to the cops, Superman gestured toward the food service van, which had apparently been stolen for the purpose of this heist.

The police officer in charge nodded gratefully. "Thanks, Superman. It's good to see you around again. Even if you don't quite . . . er, look the same."

"It's good to *be* around," Superman agreed.

Taking to the air, he banked to the side and cast a glance at the people pressing their faces to the main terminal's windows. It seemed they'd noticed him. A number of them were waving at him happily.

Behind his faceplate, he couldn't help grinning. It felt good to be on the job again, no matter what he had to wear to do it.

A flash of sunlight on glass caught his eye. Turning to a spot where the tarmac met the base of the airport building, he found himself staring into the lens of a camera. And behind the lens was Jimmy Olsen.

If someone had to get the pictures of the day, he was glad it was Jimmy. And he knew Perry White would run banner headlines with the photos.

Sighing, the Man of Steel made a beeline back to S.T.A.R. Labs. He was nearing the end of his air supply.

When Jimmy Olsen dropped a copy of the evening edition of the *Planet* on Perry White's desk, the editor gave him a nod.

"Good work, son," he said. "Those were some pictures you got of Superman. It's good to know he's back on the job, one way or the other."

"Thanks, Chief," Jimmy said, blushing a little.

"Well," said Perry, "don't just stand there patting yourself on the back. You've got to cover the mayor's speech, remember? The one about all this crime and what he's going to do about it?"

The younger man blanched as he looked at his watch. "Omigosh, you're right! I've gotta get going!"

The editor got some satisfaction out of watching Jimmy hustle. No one ever made his mark in the newspaper business *without* hustling. Thanks to Perry, the boy had learned that in a hurry.

Young Olsen was a good kid, the editor thought. He wished he had a few more like him.

Taking a sip of his coffee, he carefully unfolded

the latest edition of the *Planet* and raised it to his nose. There was something almost magical about a newspaper hot off the presses: the whiteness of the paper, the crispness of the folds, and that oh-so-special smell of fresh ink.

As always, he scanned the front page, making sure everything was exactly as he'd specified. The layout people had long ago learned not to second-guess him. He knew what sold, after all.

He was particularly proud of the headline. It read, MAN OF 'SEAL' SAVES GOLD.

"Man of Seal," he murmured aloud, then snickered a bit. It had a certain ring to it.

The story told of how thieves had tried to hijack a shipment of ancient Aztec gold headed for an exhibition at the Metropolis Museum. The reporter's description of the containment suit jibed with the tip Perry received about Superman's virus the day before.

Two of Jimmy's photos ran with the article—one of the thieves holding up the cargo handlers and one of Superman stopping their getaway van with one hand. The pictures left no doubt it was the Man of Steel in that bulky suit.

Perry set the paper down with a sigh of relief. If Superman was back, the crime wave would soon be history. He shook his head and opened the paper to page two.

In Smallville, Martha Kent sat bolt upright when the anchor mentioned a breaking story coming up about Superman. Unfortunately, commercials interrupted the news show.

"Jonathan!" she called.

Her husband came running from the kitchen, a piece of apple pie in one hand. It was his favorite—and hers—but this hardly seemed to be the time for a snack.

"How can you eat now?" she scolded. Before he could answer, she added, "Sit down, quick. There's another story coming up about Clark."

"What did they say?" he asked, sitting beside her. "And the pie's for you, dear. You need to eat. You didn't touch breakfast."

"Hmmph," she said, but accepted the plate. "They didn't say anything yet—except that it's a breaking story."

"There it is," her husband said, plunking himself down in the chair next to hers.

Not daring to take his eyes off the TV screen, Jonathan fumbled for the remote. Finding it, he turned up the sound just as the picture cut to a series of newspaper photographs. They showed Superman in some sort of bizarre, bulky outfit.

"Unconfirmed reports," the reporter was saying, "claim that Superman has been infected with a deadly, incurable disease. The special containment suit he was seen wearing in Metropolis early this morning may be an indication that the rumors are true. If so, this special suit is supposed to protect our city from him." The reporter looked deadly serious for a moment. "However, many are wondering how safe it really is."

The image changed to that of a stodgy-looking fellow with a short gray beard seated at an imposing wooden desk. He wore a white lab coat, and underneath him appeared the words, *Dr. Viktor Zakaroff, Centers for Disease Control.*

Dr. Zakaroff looked into the camera without smiling. "We really have no evidence to go on yet," he pointed out. "Nor do I wish to seem overly dramatic. However, if this virus is as deadly and easily spread as reported, it's absolutely critical that it never go beyond Superman. Personally, I would like to see him restricted to a secure quarantine facility at once."

Martha clutched Jonathan's arm in panic.

"I'm sure he's exaggerating the risk," her husband noted, trying to sound soothing, but Martha recognized the deep furrows in his brow. He was as worried as she was. And not just about Clark.

Martha also wondered about Lois. Where was she? Was she making any progress in her struggle to get to the bottom of this?

"Eat," Jonathan said softly. He put his arm around her shoulders. "It's not going to do Clark any good for you to waste away."

Reluctantly she picked up the pie again. Though her heart wasn't in it, she took a bite—and prayed for the best.

CHAPTER TEN

Professor Killgrave strode briskly into his medical theater, all thoughts of showmanship forgotten. He'd been summoned—there was no other word for it—to this emergency meeting with Smith. "Be there," his contact told him, "or we'll come to you."

So he'd come. And on the way, he'd heard the report of Superman's capture of the thieves at the airport. Then he'd understood. Those had been Smith's people.

When he walked into the medical theater, Smith was already there waiting, the usual bodyguards in tow. Smith was angry and didn't bother concealing it.

"Superman—" he began, his voice dripping with frustration.

Killgrave waved him to silence. "I knew it was only a matter of time before he figured out a way around the virus. He does have a certain cunning."

"That doesn't help my men," Smith snarled. "I lost two good people today. People I wouldn't have risked if I thought Superman might turn up."

"It's an inconvenience, nothing more," Killgrave answered, with more assurance than he felt. "We've got to stay one step ahead of our adversary, that's all. The key is his containment suit. It's a help, of course, but also a liability for him."

Smith's eyes narrowed. "Yes," he said after a moment. "You're right. The suit is his Achilles' heel. But how do we exploit that weakness? You're the genius, you figure it out." His eyes narrowed even more, giving him a decidedly sinister appearance. "One thing's for sure, Killgrave. You're not getting another penny until Superman is stopped."

The scientist dismissed the idea with a wave of his hand. "I'm not in this for the money alone," he frowned. If only he could have done this without the help of such . . . barbarians.

"Give me until tomorrow morning," the professor added. "I'll have the answer for you then."

Smith rose. "You'd better. This is costing me money. And I'm not happy when I lose money."

Then, without so much as a backward glance, he turned and walked out of the room. His men fell in step behind him.

In the doorway Smith paused. "When I'm not happy," he said without looking back, almost as an afterthought, "people die." Then he swept out.

"I could say the same thing," Killgrave chuckled, a note of menace creeping into his voice. He reached into his pocket and fingered the little laser pistol he had begun keeping there . . . in case of emergencies.

Lois pulled into Indian Path, Maine, at one o'clock in the morning, exhausted from the long drive. After a block or so, she spotted a small motel—KODIAK LODGE, the sign read, with a picture of a huge bear next to the name. Its vacancy sign was on, so she drove up to the office.

Behind the counter, a bored-looking teenager sat watching an old movie on a black-and-white TV. He had wild curly red hair, a ton of freckles, and a Red Sox sweatshirt. He barely glanced up as she came in.

"I'd like your best room," she said.

"Sure. Sign in." Without looking at Lois, he pushed an old-fashioned registration book her way.

She put down her name and the *Daily Planet*'s address.

"That'll be twenty-two dollars," the kid said. "In cash. In advance."

"Is this your best room?" she asked.

The kid grinned. "We only have one room left."

The reporter sighed. "I don't suppose there's another motel around?"

"Nope."

Lois silently counted out a twenty and two ones and slid them over the countertop. The kid turned away from the TV for the first time, put the money in the register, and only then removed a key from a peg and handed it to her. He glanced down at the registration book.

"Number eight," he said. "And the institute's two miles down on the left. They open at nine o'clock."

Lois was startled. "How did you know—?" she began.

"Easy," the kid told her. "We don't get many visitors. And now that Superman's sick, all sorts of newspeople are here to interview Mr. Plymouth. That's why we're full up, and it's not even hunting season yet."

She absorbed the information. Apparently her big lead was no longer hers alone. Somehow some of her "colleagues" in the newsgathering community had got hold of it as well.

But that didn't daunt her. All it meant was that she'd have to work twice as hard to get a scoop.

Besides, Lois was after a lot more than a story here. She was trying to save Clark.

She considered the kid behind the counter for a moment. "What's he like, this Mr. Plymouth?"

The kid's face brightened. "You going to get your camera and interview me?" he asked with a grin.

"Sorry," she said. "I work for a newspaper."

"Oh." He shrugged, his excitement dimming. "Well, he's all right, I guess. I go to school with his daughter, Mindy. She's kind of strange."

"In what way?" Lois prodded.

"You know." The kid made an eerie whistling sound. "Believes in UFOs and weird stuff."

"And you don't?"

He shook his head. "I'd have to see one first."

Not much I can get from this conversation, Lois told herself. It would be better to get some sleep and start poking around in the morning.

"Thanks," she told the kid.

Picking up her key, Lois headed for her room.

"Weight isn't a problem," Superman said, trying on the new backpack Kitty Faulkner's people had rigged for the containment suit. "I'm more concerned with aerodynamics."

It was after midnight at S.T.A.R. Labs. Dark circles lined Kitty's eyes, but she'd insisted on working late to get the suit modified to Superman's specs. Now she nodded.

"It's a valid concern," she said. "You'll have to fly more slowly until you get used to the added drag of the tanks."

Superman had asked her to find some way to increase the amount of time he could spend outside. She'd ordered larger air tanks, and they'd only just arrived. Now he would have nearly two hours' worth of oxygen before he even had to think about holding his breath—the best they could do under the circumstances.

He slipped his arms through the pack that would hold the tanks and estimated the weight at a hundred and fifty pounds. That would be enough to slow down a normal man, but with his superstrength he hardly felt it.

"It's going to work," Superman told her.

He saw her relax for the first time in about six hours. She even managed a smile.

He smiled, too. "It's going to work just fine."

The next morning, Superman left S.T.A.R. Labs at exactly seven o'clock, the two new air tanks on his back. He adjusted the flow of oxygen, then took off for a quick flight over Metropolis.

Scanning the streets below for signs of trouble, he found one almost at once. An emergency exit on top of a building in Jeweler's Row had been pried open.

The sign on the facade identified the edifice as Whitney Jewelers, one of the poshest places in town. They probably had millions of dollars' worth of merchandise in their showcases, not to mention what they kept in their vaults.

The thieves hadn't even made an effort to cover their entrance. Perhaps they hadn't yet heard Superman was back in business.

The Man of Steel landed lightly, then lowered himself through the open exit. The sophisticated electronic alarm system had been disassembled, he noticed. And a thick steel security door had been blasted off its hinges by some kind of powerful explosive.

Inside, Superman could hear the thieves chatting among themselves. While he had been taught it was rude to interrupt, he believed they would understand if he made an exception this time.

With superspeed, the Man of Steel burst in on the crooks, startling them and catching them red-handed.

The man nearest him had a thin, pinched face,

94

reminiscent of a rat's. He wore a long raincoat and in one hand held a cloth bag, into which he had been dumping trays of jewelry and cut gems taken from display cases. Three more men were working behind him.

"Sorry to ruin your fun," Superman told them, "but playtime's over."

Sighing with relief, the man in the raincoat smiled at him. "Not by a long shot, it's not." He turned to his associates. "It's okay. Just keep working."

They did as they were told. Despite Superman's presence, the men went on emptying trays of jewelry.

Surprised, the Man of Steel took a step toward the burglars. "Feeling a little cocky, aren't we?" he asked.

The man in the raincoat raised his hand. He didn't seem the least bit worried.

"Not so fast," he said. "Not unless you want to release your supervirus on the entire population of Metropolis."

Superman stopped in his tracks. "What do you mean?" he demanded. He suspected that the crook was bluffing, but he didn't want to take any chances.

The man in the raincoat pointed to a nearby counter. There, on top of a now-empty display case, sat a video camera with a wide-angle lens. An antenna jutted up from it. It was broadcasting its signal, Superman realized.

"So we have an audience," the Man of Steel said. "What does that have to do with anything?"

"This," said the crook, with obvious relish.

With a sneer, he opened his raincoat. He wore a belt of explosives around his waist.

"It's a shrapnel belt," he went on, allowing his coat to close. "If my boss sees you move one finger to stop us, he's going to blow me up. Boom!" He laughed. "And little bits of flying steel will shred that outfit you're wearing, letting loose the virus."

"But you'd be dead," Superman told him.

"I didn't say I liked the idea," the man replied. "That's why my boss isn't letting me make the call. He said he could be more *objective* about pressing the button."

Superman took a step back. "So I'm just supposed to stand here and watch you rob the place, is that it?"

"Not quite." The man smiled, clearly enjoying this immensely. "You're supposed to leave. Get lost. Beat it."

"I get the idea," Superman said through clenched teeth.

"And you can't stop us with your heat vision from a distance, either," the man went on, gloating, "or you'll melt your faceplate. So unless you want to spread the virus, my boss says you can just take a flying leap.

"And don't try following us. He'll be watching for you. And if he so much as suspects you're trying to find out where we're going, the next time you won't get a warning."

Superman bit his lip. His hands were tied, neatly and efficiently.

"Who *is* your boss?" he wondered out loud.

"You know I can't answer that," the man remarked with a grin. "But he said to tell you that he appreciates your cooperation. Got it?"

"Got it," Superman echoed.

The words were like poison to him, like gall in his mouth. But he knew he couldn't risk innocent lives, no matter what the consequences.

Reluctantly Superman ducked back out onto the roof and took to the sky. The air tanks on his back made him wobble a bit in the air, but he quickly straightened himself out.

The muscles worked savagely in his temples. He could barely contain his frustration. In a way, this was even worse than before, when he'd had no way of leaving his containment cell. Now he could *see* the crime taking place—and yet there was nothing he could do about it.

At least for now.

CHAPTER ELEVEN

Lois drove out to the Kodiak Institute for Extraterrestrial Research at 9:00 A.M.

The institute proved to be a complex of surprisingly modern-looking buildings on a large, wooded lot. As she went through the open gates, set between high brick walls topped with barbed wire, she reflected that the place looked as if it had been built to withstand a siege. All it needed was a string of gun towers.

Lois headed toward what looked like the main building and parked in a small lot, between news vans from WRED-TV 4 and WMEG-TV 63. It seemed the competition had already arrived. At least Emmett Plymouth wasn't averse to publicity, she thought.

The receptionist, an elderly woman who looked at least eighty, smiled at her as she came through the double doors. Then two security guards converged on her.

They were both carrying metal detectors, which they passed over her body. The devices began to beep when they came near her purse. One of the guards tried to take the purse from Lois, but she clutched it more tightly.

"Excuse me," Lois said, "but what do you think you're doing?"

"Routine check," one of the guards told her. "Dr. Plymouth's orders. Nobody gets in here unless they're thoroughly checked. That includes all purses, handbags, and equipment."

Lois drew a deep breath, about to launch into a heated argument. Then she thought better of it.

She sighed and surrendered to the indignity of having her purse dumped out onto a plastic tray. She kept a careful eye on the guard as he poked through her possessions with the eraser end of a pencil.

This is for Clark, she had to remind herself over and over, folding her arms defiantly. For Clark, who's penned up in that awful containment chamber like a lab rat. He's the only reason I'm putting up with this.

Finally the guard returned her purse. "It's okay," he said to the receptionist. "Nothing of alien origin in there."

"Alien origin?" the reporter asked.

"That's right," the elderly woman said matter-of-factly. "They know Doc Plymouth is studying them, and they're always trying to sneak something past us."

Lois bit her tongue. Obviously these people were off the wall. But they could also be an important link in her investigation. For now, she would have to tolerate their eccentricities.

"Now, how may I help you?" the receptionist asked, as if nothing out of the ordinary had taken place.

Keep calm, Lois told herself. *At least until you get what you came for.*

"I'm Lois Lane, from the *Daily Planet*," she said. "I'd like to see the director."

The receptionist consulted an open date book on her desk. "Doc Plymouth has a very busy schedule today."

"I saw all the TV trucks outside," Lois noted.

"He's giving two interviews this morning," the woman told her. "Maybe we could squeeze you in afterward. We don't get many newspaper people up here, you know."

I can't imagine why, Lois thought. But of course, she didn't say it out loud.

"You can take a seat over there," the receptionist said, pointing to a couch across from her desk. There were a few magazines on a table next to it. "I'll call you."

"Thank you," Lois replied.

She crossed over and took a seat. The magazines were all back issues of *Sky and Telescope* and *Astronomy*, not a *Newstime* in sight. Sighing, she picked one up and flipped through it to look at the pictures. She had a feeling this was going to take a while.

And all the time, Clark would be languishing in his cold, antiseptic prison.

Just after eleven o'clock, the receptionist called. "Honey? Honey?"

Lois looked up. "The name," she said, controlling her exasperation, "is Lois Lane."

"Lois, honey," the woman amended, "Doc

Plymouth's got a fifteen-minute break and can see you now. The third door on the left."

"Thanks," Lois told her.

She got up. If she never looked at another issue of *Sky and Telescope*, it would be too soon.

A man was waiting for her inside a large conference room. If this was Plymouth, she reflected, he was nothing like she'd imagined.

Rather than a mousy little scientist with thick glasses and a pocket protector filled with pens, he was a tall, deeply tanned, muscular man in a suit and tie. He flashed her a dazzling smile and rose to meet her.

"Lois Lane!" he said in a rich, deep baritone. "I'm Dr. Emmett Plymouth. Please call me Doc; everyone else does. I'm delighted to make your acquaintance. Of course, I've read a number of your stories on the Superman hoax."

Lois looked at him, sincerely taken aback. Was he joking?

"You think he's a hoax?" she asked.

Plymouth nodded. "Have a seat," he said. When she was seated, he sat opposite her. "I've been following Superman's spectacular career with interest for some time, you know. I subscribe to a number of clipping services, which provide me with stories from local and national papers about aliens, UFOs, and the like. I've often seen your name—and that of a Mr. Clark Kent—linked with Superman's."

"We've been fortunate enough to get a number of stories about him," Lois said a little uncomfortably.

"So now you're finally here to debunk the hoax," he said, obviously jumping to the wrong conclusion. "That's wonderful. And yes, before you ask, I do have definitive proof that it is a hoax—which is, of course, what's drawn all the media attention. I like to give the locals a bit of a scoop whenever I can—though I don't expect them to wield the kind of influence you can. Let me get my files. I'll be right back."

Lois nodded. "Sure," she said.

Apparently, she thought as he left the room, Plymouth wasn't the only one who had jumped to the wrong conclusion. It seemed the other reporters here were just rising to the doctor's bait about the "hoax," not pursuing the Virus X angle.

Interesting. But it made it all the more critical that she focus on what she'd come for.

A minute later, Doc Plymouth returned and seated himself opposite her. He had a thick red folder with SUPERMAN printed across the front.

"Here," he said, pulling out a glossy black-and-white photo and sliding it across to her. "Take a look at this and tell me what you think it is."

It was a hokey "UFO alien" picture from one of the tabloid newspapers—an alien with a scrawny body, thin neck, huge bald head, and large, unblinking black eyes.

"An artist's conception of an alien?" she asked hesitantly.

"This," said Doc Plymouth with pride, "is the *real* Superman. The one you know is an impostor. They replaced this Superman with the bogus one a few years ago, as part of a covert CIA operation called 'Michelangelo.' All the details are here."

He patted the folder. "The whole Superman thing is a hoax. And now the CIA is claiming he has an incurable disease so the actor posing as Superman can retire."

"I see," Lois said. It took a real effort not to laugh. The whole idea was absurd . . . and blatantly untrue. But he still might be able to help her.

"Actually," she managed to add after a minute, "I'm not here on the Superman story, which has got pretty old in Metropolis."

"No?" he said. His brow wrinkled in puzzlement. "Then why?"

"It's something entirely different," Lois explained. "I'm looking for any alien life-forms that came to Earth recently. Not necessarily sentient beings. Even viruses, microbes, or bacteria would—"

Plymouth eyed her. "Ah," he said. "You're referring to that article, then."

"Article?" she repeated.

"You haven't seen it?"

She shook her head. "What was it about?"

The director shrugged. "About a month and a half ago, a meteorite was stolen from a private research lab in New Mexico. Apparently the scientist working on the meteorite was murdered during the robbery.

"Of course," Plymouth went on, "it was never considered a big enough story to make the news here in the east, although it headlined in the Santa Fe *Examiner*. But the claim was that the meteorite contained some kind of alien life-form. Something microscopic."

"The Santa Fe *Examiner*," Lois mused. "Do you still have the article? I'd love to get a copy."

"It's somewhere, but I'm afraid I couldn't get my hands on it," he told her. "Alien life-forms don't travel in meteors, so it wouldn't be in any of my usual files. Besides, my work here is focused on saving Earth from the threat of alien invasion, and microbes are not a factor in that— no matter *what* H. G. Wells would have us believe."

She knew the reference. *The War of the Worlds*.

Lois leaned forward. "How about the name of the lab where the theft took place?"

Plymouth sighed. "It was the Santa Fe something-or-other Labs, I think. Why are you so concerned about it?"

"Well," she said, "I'm working on a story about researchers splicing alien DNA into terrestrial life-forms." It was a lie, of course, but she wasn't going to let it leak out that she was on the verge of solving Superman's problem. It might make her job more complicated. "I think a group of criminals is trying to create a hybrid of some kind."

"Ah," the director said, his eyes brightening. Apparently this was right up his alley. "That does sound serious. I wish you good luck in finding and exposing them." He touched an intercom button on the desk. "Miss Hawthorne," he said, "Lois Lane is leaving now. Please have security escort her to her car."

"Of course, Doc," old Miss Hawthorne replied. "They'll be right there."

Lois rose. The interview seemed at an end.

"I hope I've been of some help," said Plymouth.

She nodded. "You've been a *big* help."

Lois's reporter instincts told her she was on the right track. Now all she had to do was find that article.

Superman was just emerging from S.T.A.R. Labs in his containment suit when a radio bulletin caught his attention.

"The top story," the reporter said, "is a bomb threat at the Chesterville Mall in Chesterton Township. An anonymous caller phoned this station telling us that the bomb is set to go off sometime in the next several minutes—and that it's up to Superman to find it before it's too late. Police are already investigating the report, but no confirmation—"

Superman didn't wait to hear any more. He

understood that this was some kind of diversion, designed to draw his attention away from something else. But that didn't help him much.

He couldn't let innocent people die, no matter the circumstances. Changing direction in midair, he sped off toward the mall.

Lois drove straight back to the Kodiak Lodge. She didn't have to check out of her room until three o'clock, which left her nearly an hour. Her phone call to that laboratory in New Mexico wouldn't take nearly that long.

She dialed Santa Fe directory information, found only one laboratory that seemed to match Doc Plymouth's vague name—the Santa Fe Environmental Research Labs—and jotted down the number. Then she called it.

On the second ring, a male voice answered. "Santa Fe Labs."

"Hello," she said. "My name is Lois Lane, and I'm calling from the *Daily Planet* in Metropolis. Do you have a publicist or someone I could speak with?"

"I'll put you through to Mrs. Williamson," he said. "Please hold."

The phone rang again, and this time a woman with a warm southern accent picked up. "This is Mrs. Williamson. How may I help you?"

"This is Lois Lane from the *Daily Planet* in Metropolis," the reporter told her. "I'm working on a story that may relate to the theft of a meteorite from your facility. Is there someone I can talk to about it? The director, perhaps?"

"That would be me," Mrs. Williamson said. "Did you see the story in the *Examiner*? It contained all the information we have for the general public."

"Unfortunately, I didn't," Lois replied. "But I just have a few questions."

"I'll help if I can, of course," the woman assured her.

"About the man who was murdered—"

"Dr. Valdez," said Mrs. Williamson.

"Valdez?" Lois jotted that down on the notepad beside the phone.

"But he wasn't murdered," the woman noted. "He killed himself."

Really, thought the reporter. "Maybe you'd better start at the beginning," she suggested.

The woman sighed. "Last summer, José Valdez, our previous director of research, found a meteorite in the desert. From his notes, the police learned that he had been secretly trying to sell it to an old college roommate. It seems he believed the meteorite contained alien DNA of some kind. We haven't been able to confirm this information since the thing was stolen."

"Very interesting," Lois said, writing frantically. "Go on."

"Apparently, this old roommate was a convicted felon, but also a brilliant scientist in several different fields. Valdez thought his friend would make a lot of money for them from this alien-DNA discovery, although nobody has been able to figure out how.

"Valdez met with his friend, gave him a tour of the facility, and then they left together with the meteorite. Valdez's body turned up several days later. He'd killed himself in a motel in Chicago, though some say it was homicide . . . and I'm afraid that's all we know."

"You wouldn't happen to know the roommate's name by any chance?" asked Lois.

The director thought for a moment. "Killgrave," she said at last. "Professor Thaddeus Killgrave."

Lois gasped. Killgrave!

He was the scientific genius Superman had run into a couple of times before. Once Killgrave had used nuclear weapons to try to extort money from Metropolis. But of course the Man of Steel had stopped him.

And the scientist had had it in for Superman ever since.

Killgrave had to be the one behind the contamination plot. It sounded like something he would come up with.

"Thank you," Lois said. "That's all I needed to know."

"You're welcome," Mrs. Williamson said.

Lois hung up, still thinking. If Killgrave were the one behind this virus, and he'd developed it from the alien DNA he'd found, it was a good bet he'd come up with the cure as well. After all, what if he were accidentally exposed to the disease?

Now all I've got to do is find him, she told herself. But where do you go to look for a mad scientist?

CHAPTER TWELVE

Shorty Capistrano was anything but short. In point of fact, he was six feet six, with immense shoulders and hands the size of hubcaps.

But it wasn't his size that made him one of Smith's most prized operatives. It was his intelligence.

The same intelligence that allowed him to appreciate the artfulness with which his boss had orchestrated things. The phone calls to all the radio and TV stations in Metropolis, for instance—they'd gone out at 11:55 in the morning, just in time to make the noon broadcasts.

Superman wouldn't be able to stop this next crime. He'd be too busy checking out Chesterville Mall.

Chuckling, Shorty continued his slow march through the sewers beneath Metropolis, his men right behind him. One of Smith's operatives had already come through here, scouting the way, and glow-in-the-dark chalk marked the passages they were to take.

Shorty glanced over his shoulder and saw his "assistants" following close behind. Like him, Red, Jones, and Phelps were dressed in black rubber scuba-diving suits. And, also like him, they were pros—the only type that Smith was likely to employ.

The sewer opened up ahead, at a small junction

with a steel grating overhead. A large X marked the spot.

Sewer workers—or, rather, men posing as sewer workers—had installed a copper pipe here the week before. It ran on an angle, heading up and out of sight through the concrete wall.

This, Shorty knew, was the spot. It was exactly as Smith had described it.

Unclipping a small canister from his belt, he fitted it onto the open end of the copper pipe and pushed a small button. The hiss of escaping gases told him the device was functioning properly, pumping huge doses of chloroform knockout gas up the pipe and into a large private residence in the heart of Metropolis.

As the pump worked, Shorty pulled a gas mask from his belt and put it on. Instantly the stink of the sewer vanished, replaced by the sharp chemical smell of fresh plastic. But he could breathe fine.

Steel rungs set into the wall under the grating provided handholds. Shorty began to climb. When he got to the top, he pushed the grate up and to the side, then climbed out into a private garden.

It was actually located inside the house, Shorty marveled. Lush flowers bloomed all around him, in shades of red and yellow and pink. The ceiling, made of glass, admitted bright sunshine.

The gas seemed to have done its job. There

were two ferocious-looking guard dogs—huge, muscular Dobermans—fast asleep to the left of the grating. Their feet twitched now and then, but that was it.

Turning, Shorty helped the other three up and out. When they were all in the courtyard, they unzipped their scuba-diving suits and peeled them away.

They were dressed in jeans, white tennis shirts, and sneakers. From the pack one of the men had been carrying, Shorty drew out large plastic bags with airtight seals. Some were as much as ten feet around. They would protect the loot when the men took it back out through the sewers.

Next, Shorty passed out hand-drawn maps of the house from his front pocket. He didn't know how Smith had got them, but he knew they were accurate.

Each one showed where a few particularly valuable treasures were kept. Silently, and with practiced certainty, the men spread out to accomplish their various tasks.

Shorty's map led him through the kitchens, where four cooks and two assistants had been busy preparing supper. Now they slumped across the tables, counters, and floor, unconscious. Carefully Shorty turned off the ovens and stoves; no sense risking anyone's death or injury due to a fire. He and his men were thieves, not murderers.

He came out into the dining room, then went into the study. At a huge marble-topped desk before an immense granite fireplace, Mr. Felix Gottsworthy sat slumped.

Shorty chuckled. Gottsworthy was one of the wealthiest men in Metropolis, and his passion was collecting fine art. An original Rembrandt hung on the wall behind the desk.

Taking it down, Shorty dismantled the frame, then rolled the painting up gingerly. Turning, he carried it to the garden room and stowed it safely inside a sealed plastic bag. After checking his map, he fetched two more paintings by Old World masters.

Just some canvas and paint, he thought wryly. But these few paintings alone would make their haul one of the biggest in Metropolis history. And they weren't done yet—far from it.

The others had all finished with their "errands" by the time he got back with a large Renoir painting of a woman pouring milk from a pitcher. Most people thought there was only one such Renoir, hanging in a famous European museum. But Smith knew that Renoir had done an almost identical work for a friend.

The garden room looked like a rummage sale, with small statues, paintings, two fancy Louis XIV chairs, and a box of diamond and gold jewelry assembled there, all zipped safely into transparent plastic bags.

The robbers put their rubber suits back on.

Then Shorty pulled up the grate. As his men climbed down into the sewers, Shorty began passing plastic bags to them. When everything had been safely lowered, the big man checked his watch.

Twenty-two minutes, he thought, satisfied. The whole heist had only taken twenty-two minutes. As he looked over the treasures they'd gathered, he tried to estimate how many millions of dollars' worth of artwork and jewelry they'd taken.

Thirty million? Forty? He had no idea.

In another couple of minutes, they would disappear into the sewer tunnels and split up. There were so many tunnels, so many twists and turns and branchings, the police could never hope to search them all. If one of them got caught, it'd be a crime-fighting miracle—but the rest of them would escape.

And somewhere in Chesterton, Superman was still trying to defuse the bomb Killgrave had devised. Shorty began to chuckle.

Yes, it was a good day all the way around. Still chuckling, he and his men picked up their loot and headed down the tunnel, back the way they'd come.

A sudden movement ahead caught Shorty's eye. He drew up short. There was a figure up ahead in the shadows of the tunnel, watching them.

A man in a white containment suit. Who else could it be but Superman?

Just as Shorty thought this, the figure ducked to the side, out of sight. The thief began to curse under his breath. How had Superman disposed of the bomb so quickly?

Well, he might have found them, but Shorty still had a trump card—the threat of releasing the virus. All he had to do was make it clear to Superman that he was endangering his containment suit, and he'd have to get out of their way.

The thief tucked the paintings more tightly under his arm and drew his gun, a .38 revolver. He cocked it in one swift motion. The sound of the hammer locking into place seemed a hundred times louder than usual. Then he heard the sound repeated by his men.

"Fire," Shorty rasped.

As he pulled the trigger, the others did the same. The tunnel lit up with the flashes of their weapons and the sparks made by bullets ricocheting off stone.

Shorty gestured for them to stop. The tunnel went silent.

"Let's make a break for it," Shorty whispered, keeping his eye on the darkness ahead. "Just remember to keep firing. Superman won't want to risk that containment suit, and our bullets can cut it to shreds."

"Gotcha," said his men.

"Red," he began, turning to Red McCoy—but the man was gone. He blinked in surprise. "Where's Red?" he demanded.

Phelps and Jones looked just as bewildered as Shorty was.

"He was right beside me a minute ago," Jones said.

Shorty scowled. Maybe Red had panicked and run. But he couldn't worry about that now.

"Okay, here's the plan," he said. He looked up the sewer tunnel toward the spot where he'd last glimpsed Superman. "Phelps—"

"Uh—Shorty," Jones said.

"What?" he demanded, glancing back.

Then Shorty saw that Phelps was gone, too. It was just him and Jones now. He swallowed the knot that he suddenly felt in his throat.

"Where'd Phelps go?" Shorty asked.

"I don't know," Jones said, a hysterical note creeping into his voice. "He was right here! I looked away for a second, and he disappeared!"

"That's impossible," Shorty said, trying to sound confident.

Both Red and Phelps had taken off down one of the other tunnels, that's all. He glanced again at the place where he'd seen Superman.

"Just stick with me," he told Jones. "I'll get us out of this. You hear me? Jones? *Jones?*"

Shorty felt a chill sweep through him. Turning slowly, he saw that he was alone. Jones, too, had vanished.

Then, before Shorty could move, the gun was plucked from his hand and twisted into scrap metal. And suddenly, Superman was standing before him. Apparently he'd moved so fast in the near darkness that Shorty hadn't been able to see him.

"Leave me alone," the crook snapped. "Or my boss'll release the virus, I swear it!"

"Swear all you want," the Man of Steel countered. "I've got a feeling you're lying. Not even a thief wants to risk ravaging the world. And since you haven't got a remote-controlled shrapnel belt on, I don't have to worry about anyone having an itchy trigger finger."

Shorty cursed beneath his breath. They had considered his wearing the shrapnel belt but scrapped the idea because remote control wasn't possible down in these old tunnels.

"Then again," Superman went on, "feel free to tell the police all about it. They're standing right behind you."

"You're the one who's lying now," Shorty said.

"Am I?" asked his adversary.

Abruptly Shorty felt the barrel of a pistol being pressed into the small of his back.

"That's right," a voice said behind him. "You have the right to remain silent . . ." The officer continued reading him his rights under the law.

Shorty just stared at Superman's face through the containment suit mask. "You won't get away with this," he promised.

Superman grinned. "I think I already have—with a little help from my friends."

The cop pulled Shorty's arms behind his back and handcuffed him. That's when the thief turned and saw that the cop, too, was wearing a containment suit.

Superman nodded with satisfaction as he stood in the shadow of the Gottsworthy mansion and watched the police take the last of the thieves away. It wasn't just that he'd foiled another heist. He felt as if he had a handle on this crime wave again—as if he were in control.

At least for now.

Fortunately he had located the bomb in the mall in less than a minute, using his X-ray vision. Rather than waste precious time trying to defuse it, he'd picked it up and flown as high as he could. Then, using all the strength at his disposal, he'd hurled it into the upper atmosphere, where it exploded harmlessly.

Then he had called his friend Dan Turpin of the Metropolis Special Crimes Unit and asked him to see if any major crimes had been reported in the city. Turpin had checked—and reported that a silent alarm had gone off at the Gottsworthy estate.

That was on the other side of Metropolis from the mall—exactly the way one would have planned it, if one wanted Superman out of the way.

Of course, the Man of Steel could simply have allowed the police to respond. And in fact, they were in the process of doing so when he got involved.

But this was a dangerous job for regular cops—and a ridiculously difficult one. There were too many tunnels to worry about, too many places for criminals to conceal themselves. And a firefight in such tight quarters would have wound up with some brave officer getting killed.

Superman couldn't allow that.

But by the same token, he couldn't risk a stray bullet hitting his S.T.A.R. Labs garb, not while he was at the mercy of this virus.

So he had picked Turpin up, stopped just long enough to acquire a containment suit from the police labs, and headed for the Gottsworthy estate. Then he placed Turpin in the tunnel right under the mansion, in the hope that the thieves would mistake him for Superman.

With a containment suit on, the cop was likely to pass muster—at least in the dark and at a distance. And if Turpin was careful, he'd slow the thieves down without placing himself in any great danger.

Then Superman could sneak around behind them and pick them off one by one. What's more, the plan had worked like a charm.

"Hey, Big Blue!" bellowed Turpin.

Superman turned to see the cop approaching. Turpin had removed his helmet, exposing his rough, craggy features, but he still wore the rest of his containment suit.

119

"Thanks, Dan," said the Man of Tomorrow. "I couldn't have done it without you."

"Yeah, right," the cop chuckled, dismissing the idea with a wave of his hand. "So, any luck with a cure yet?"

Superman shook his head ruefully. "Afraid not."

Turpin laid a hand on the shoulder of his friend's suit. "It'll happen. Just hang in there, okay?"

Superman smiled. "Okay," he agreed. "See you later, Dan."

The cop nodded. "Yeah. Later."

As the Man of Steel walked away from the squad cars parked outside Gottworthy's house, he noticed that a crowd of interested neighbors and passersby had gathered, drawn by the sight of the police. A uniformed cop was holding them back.

But in the lurid illumination of the police car's emergency lights, Superman could see fear in people's eyes as he approached. Not fear of the crooks, he realized, but fear of him. Nor did he need his superhearing to understand what they were saying to one another.

"Look, it's Superman!"

"And he's wearing that awful suit."

"They say he's got a virus that could kill us all!"

"They ought to keep him locked up somewhere, so he can't hurt anybody."

"He's a menace—a danger to everyone."

"Shoot him into space or something."

"Get him out of here!"

Those weren't the only comments. There were expressions of sympathy, compassion, even pity. But the majority looked at him as a threat.

How ironic. He'd spent his whole adult life preserving the fabric of society. Now he himself was a hazard to it.

Without a word, he took off and headed back to S.T.A.R. Labs.

In his suite of rooms at the posh Metropolis Arms, Smith was grinding his teeth together as he watched the WGBS news team cover the botched burglary at the Gottsworthy estate.

"Superman was the key," said a police officer on the scene. "Without him, we would have had to ferret the burglars out of those tunnels, and risk police lives in the process. And that would've been some job, let me tell you."

"Jeez," said one of Smith's higher-ranking thugs, a squarish man named Rodriguez.

The other two men in the room, Smith's bodyguards, kept their mouths shut. It was smart of them, too. Whatever they might have said would have been the wrong thing.

Turning back to the television, Smith ground his teeth even harder. Clearly, this Metropolis campaign had become a disaster—a costly disaster. He decided then and there to give up on it.

"We're done here," he told Rodriguez.

"Done?" his lieutenant echoed. He looked at Smith. "As in we're leaving Metropolis?"

"That's right," said Smith.

"But what about Killgrave?" asked his lieutenant.

Smith gave a little shrug. "If he can't stop Superman like he promised, he's no longer of any use to us. But since he can identify us, he's a problem we need to deal with."

Rodriguez nodded. He had taken care of such "problems" for Smith before. Usually, the solution involved a long swim in a deep river.

Suddenly Smith heard a strange, hissing sound. He got up and looked around the room for the source.

"What is that?" he asked Rodriguez.

The squarish man shook his head. "Dunno."

Smith followed the sound. It seemed to be coming from the closet, he thought. A moment later, a pale yellow gas began seeping from under the closet door.

"Open that door, Carl," he said to one of his bodyguards, taking a step back.

The man drew a white silk handkerchief from his pocket and covered his nose. Then he swung open the double doors.

The gas was coming from inside his briefcase, Smith saw, steaming out from the seams. Someone—Killgrave?—had planted something inside it when he wasn't looking.

Carl, catching a whiff of the gas through the handkerchief over his nose, gave a low whimper and fell to one side. He twitched once, then lay still.

Rodriguez collapsed next, then Smith's other bodyguard.

The gangster himself didn't wait for the gas to reach him. Turning, he ran for the door, tore it open, and sprinted for the elevators. Frantically he punched the call buttons.

The elevator doors didn't open, though. He glanced back over his shoulder. He could still hear the hiss of escaping gas from his room.

Then just as the elevator bell rang and its doors started to open, he smelled something light, sweet, almost flowery. Everything started to go dark.

His last realization, as he fell to the carpeted floor, was that Killgrave had just handed him to the cops on a silver platter.

Back in his operating theater, Professor Killgrave pounded the table with his fists. "Betrayed!" he rasped. "Betrayed again! Why does everyone always betray me?"

At his last meeting with Smith, he had taken the opportunity to plant both a bug and a miniature gas canister in the briefcase's inside pocket. After all, he wanted to be able to keep tabs on Smith. He needed to know what the man was planning.

Killgrave had had a feeling that Smith would turn against him at some point. And he had been right to be suspicious, hadn't he? Unfortunately, he was always right about such things.

Why were people always trying to pull the wool over his eyes? he wondered. Why were they always exploiting him, sucking him dry, stabbing him in the back?

Again Killgrave pounded the table. "Why?" he shrieked. "Why, why, why?"

The theater echoed savagely with his cries. As they died down, he raised his chin slowly and deliberately, facing the observation gallery as if addressing an imaginary class.

"Once more," he said, his voice deadly quiet, "Superman has outlasted me. Smith was the instrument of my revenge. Without him, I've no way to strike at the Man of Steel for all the trouble he's caused me."

Killgrave removed his glasses and cleaned them on the front of his lab coat. Then he replaced them on the bridge of his nose.

"Money was never my goal in this," he explained. "Oh, it would have paid for a substantial amount of research. But my true goal was always Superman's downfall. And now I have been deprived of—"

Suddenly Killgrave realized that there was still a way to beat Superman. Still a way to obtain his full measure of revenge. And not just on the Man of Tomorrow. No, he could have his revenge on . . .

. . . *everyone*.

He began to chuckle. He knew just where to start. It would take some planning, but he could do it. Oh yes, he could do it, all right.

But first, Killgrave had a bit of unfinished business. He went to the wall, picked up the telephone handset, and dialed the police department. He knew that his special security devices would make sure the call could not be traced.

"Fifteenth precinct," a man's voice answered. "Sergeant Gaetano speaking."

"I wish to report the whereabouts of some criminals," Killgrave said. "Specifically, those who engineered the Whitney Jewelers robbery, the attempted burglary of the Felix Gottsworthy mansion, and the attempted robbery of the Aztec treasures at the airport."

"Hold on," said the police officer. "You know where these people are?"

"I do," the scientist told him. "They are in and about room 1521 at the Metropolis Arms. And you will be pleased to hear that they are also unconscious."

"Who is this?" Gaetano demanded.

"I," said Killgrave, "am the cooperative citizen who gassed them into unconsciousness for you."

Then he hung up. *Now*, he thought, *let's see the police earn their pay*. His knockout gas only lasted six hours.

Then again, police efficiency wouldn't matter soon. Nothing would matter—because there would be no one left alive it could matter to.

Killgrave laughed a hideous, cackling laugh. The world would be sorry it ever trifled with Thaddeus Killgrave!

CHAPTER THIRTEEN

After checking out of the Kodiak Lodge, Lois drove south on I-95, wondering what her next move should be. She had to find Killgrave.

Who might know his whereabouts? Whom might he associate with, besides criminals?

Criminals . . .

Suddenly she had an idea. After all, Superman had put Killgrave behind bars for a while. The scientist must have had a cellmate while he was incarcerated in the prison on Stryker's Island.

Lois knew the warden there; she'd done a series of stories on the prison the year before—stories that had been instrumental in getting him additional staff and funding. He owed her a favor for that. It was time to call it in.

Pulling out her cellular phone, she looked up the prison's number in her notebook and placed the call. Five minutes later, she had Warden Bailey on the phone.

"Lois!" he said, sounding a thousand miles away. The connection was bad; the receiver *brrrrrd* and whistled for a second, then cleared up. "What can I do for you?"

"I need a favor," she told him. "Have you turned up anything new with regard to Thaddeus Killgrave's whereabouts?"

Bailey sighed. "Unfortunately, we haven't—not since he skipped his parole." A pause. "You haven't heard anything, have you?"

"Nothing concrete," Lois replied, telling the truth. "At least, not yet. But if I find anything out, you'll be the first to know. I was hoping I could talk to one of his old cellmates—"

"No such thing," the warden told her. "Killgrave had his own cell."

She bit her lip. Of course. She should have thought of that.

"Was he friendly with anyone?"

There was silence for a moment. "I saw him talking with Spider Musgrove once or twice," Bailey recalled. "Musgrove's still here, too. You weren't thinking of talking to him, were you?"

"That's exactly what I was thinking," Lois confessed. "Even the slightest clue would be welcome at this point."

"Musgrove's a pretty rough fellow . . ."

"It's important," she emphasized. "I really need to talk to him, Warden."

She knew Bailey didn't like the idea. Still, he gave his consent.

"I'll arrange it," he said. "Nine o'clock tomorrow morning?"

"I'll be there," she promised.

A mean-looking man with a scar down the left side of his face was waiting for Lois in the visitors' area. She slid into the little booth opposite him and gazed through a sheet of bulletproof glass into the eyes of a killer: small, black, and intense. His head had been shaved; a tattoo on the back of his left hand showed a black widow spider.

Slowly, he looked her over. Lois didn't like the feeling. His eyes seemed to be dissecting her. She shivered against her will.

"I'm Lois Lane," she said.

The prisoner smiled crookedly. "Spider Musgrove."

"What are you in for?" she asked.

"Do I know you?" he said.

"No," she admitted. "I'm a reporter."

He leaned back and laced his fingers behind his head. His eyes locked with hers.

"I like fires," he said.

"What?" Lois blinked.

"I'm in because I like fires," he said evenly. "Like starting them, anyway."

Inwardly, Lois was disgusted. But she maintained a straight face.

"I'm here," she said, "because I'm trying to find Thaddeus Killgrave. I believe you knew him."

Musgrove shrugged. "The dwarf? A little. Quiet guy, real intense. But smart, you know?"

"I know," she said. "He has information I need. Can you help me find him?"

The prisoner grunted. "Why should I?"

Lois smiled sweetly. "Warden Bailey's a close friend of mine. Any help you can give me will no doubt support your parole efforts."

That meant something to him. "I guess it can't

hurt," he said a little reluctantly. "I don't know much, though. And what I do know, I already told the cops."

"That's all right," said Lois. "Tell me anyway."

That smile again. "Say please," he told her.

"Say good-bye to your parole," she replied, without a hint of malice in her voice.

She had got his attention. "All right, all right," he said. "But like I told you, I don't know much. Even when the guy talked, I didn't understand a whole lot of what he was saying. It was scientific stuff. Like he was some sort of genius or something."

Lois frowned. "Did he ever talk about his past? People he liked . . . or places, maybe?"

"He didn't seem to like much of anybody," Musgrove told her. "He said people were jealous of him because of his brains. But a couple of times, he told me about college . . ."

The reporter leaned a little closer. "College?"

The prisoner nodded. "Yeah. Lots of professors hated him, he said, because he was smarter than they were. They finally forced him to drop out." He chuckled. "But he got even with them."

"How?" Lois asked.

"He found some way to bankrupt the place. They were all fired." Musgrove laughed like it was some sort of great joke.

Lois had the feeling she was on to something. "Where *did* Killgrave go to college?"

130

Of course, she could have asked the warden that question. But she wanted to see if Musgrove knew the answer—if Killgrave had thought it important enough to mention.

The prisoner thought for a moment. Then he snapped his fingers.

"Burnley," he said at last. "I remember because it seemed like such a funny name."

"Funny?" she asked. "Why's that?"

He smiled. "Burnley. Get it? Burn-ley? Me, I would've torched the place. But then I'm not a scientist-type like Killgrave, you know?"

"I know," Lois said, standing. "Thanks. You've been a help."

"What about my parole?" he said.

"I'll see what I can do," she replied.

Outside, she shuddered. But at least Musgrove had been of some help. Burnley College . . . it was a place to start.

Killgrave found the article he was looking for on page two of the *Daily Planet*'s morning edition. He chuckled to himself.

The article said that Smith had been arrested and charged with a long string of crimes. Apparently he was wanted in half a dozen states. No surprise there.

Killgrave nodded. The time had come to put the next stage of his plan into operation.

He phoned the *Planet* promptly at 9:00 A.M. and said, "Let me speak to the managing editor."

"Name?" asked the receptionist.

"Killgrave," he snapped back. "Thaddeus Killgrave."

A moment later, someone else got on. A newsroom reporter, Killgrave guessed.

"Mr. White is very busy," the woman told him. "If you'd care to leave your name and number—"

"No, I will *not* leave my name and number!" he yelled. "I'm the one who infected Superman with a supervirus. I'm the one who turned Smith and his lackeys over to the police last night . . . and I'm the one who will turn the whole of Metropolis into a wasteland tonight! Now let me speak to Perry White!"

"O-of course, sir," the reporter said, a noticeable tremor in her voice.

Killgrave fumed as he waited. Then, in short order, a deeper, masculine voice answered, "Perry White here."

"Thaddeus Killgrave," he said, reveling in the importance he knew his name would command with the *Planet* editor.

There was silence for a moment. Then, "What can I do for you, Mr. Killgrave?"

"I just wanted to let you know," said the scientist, "I'm sick of Superman, I'm sick of this city, and most especially, I'm sick of humanity. There's no loyalty left in this world, no respect for great accomplishments. As a result, I've decided to kill everyone in Metropolis."

"Kill everyone!?" White exclaimed. "How?"

Killgrave smiled. "You do, of course, know of the virus with which I infected Superman? Well, I'm going to release it at noon."

"But that's crazy," White said. "If you kill everyone, what's left for you?"

"What's left for me?" Killgrave began to laugh. "Everything!"

Then he hung up.

Half an hour later, Kitty Faulkner burst into the room on the other side of the transparent barrier from Superman. Something was up, the Man of Steel thought.

He rose from his cot, where he'd been resting. After he'd foiled the Gottsworthy burglary, the crime wave in Metropolis seemed to have slowed to a trickle.

Kitty had an anxious, almost fearful expression on her face. "What's wrong?" he asked through the intercom.

"I just got a call from Perry White," she said. "The man who infected you . . . he called the *Daily Planet* and confessed."

Superman was glad he had thought to alert Perry to his whereabouts.

"Who was it?" Superman held his breath.

"Thaddeus Killgrave."

The Man of Steel nodded; that made a certain amount of sense. Killgrave had the genius to design the virus, and he certainly had a grudge to settle with Superman. But why would he confess? Just to gloat?

"He's decided to destroy Metropolis," Kitty said. "He claims he's going to release the virus at noon. What can we do?"

"Did he say where he's going to release it?" Superman asked.

She shook her head. "No. All he gave was the time."

Superman knew that Killgrave was just nutty enough to go through with his threat. And noon . . . that was less than two hours away. He'd have to hurry.

"I'll have to stop him," he said. He crossed the room and began pulling on his containment suit.

With an entire city to cover, he knew he'd be hard-pressed to find Killgrave in time.

At ten-thirty on the nose, Killgrave pulled on a light jacket and a baseball cap, slung a camera bag over his shoulder, and walked out of the medical school building on the old Burnley College campus.

It looked nothing like the busy hall of higher learning it had been fifteen years ago, when Killgrave was a student here. Then the tree-lined paths had been packed with students and teachers hurrying to class.

Now it was completely deserted. Weeds grew everywhere; windows of the buildings were knocked out and doors boarded over.

Killgrave had bankrupted the school just to get even with his professors. They'd been jealous of his genius and tried to steer him away from his true talents.

He'd had his revenge, though. They were all out of work. And now he was walking its abandoned grounds, king of all he surveyed.

Most of the medical school's equipment had still been there in storage, and it had been an easy thing to get it set up again. Using solar power and tapping illegally into the cellular phone network had given him access to the utilities he needed.

Indeed, the school made an excellent secret base of operations. Who would suspect it?

One of the city buses still stopped at the corner, and as Killgrave stood there waiting impatiently, he reflected on the foolishness of mankind. Had people recognized his genius, had they given him the recognition and rewards he was due, he could have been their savior. He could have led them down a path of scientific discovery unequaled in the annals of history.

Now, though, he had to teach them a lesson. The virus would do quite nicely.

Very soon, Killgrave knew, they'd all regret spurning and betraying him. He began to smile. How they'd beg him for the cure, how they'd plead and bargain and offer him anything and everything.

And how he'd laugh as he denied it to them.

The bus pulled up. Its doors opened. Killgrave climbed on board, dropping six quarters into the slot, then found a seat.

He gazed reflectively out the window. His college professors should see him now, he thought.

Reaching into his pocket, he fingered the little vial containing the deadly virus. He was master of the world . . . and he held the fate of all humanity in the palm of his hand.

CHAPTER FOURTEEN

Lois had been listening to the radio all the way from the prison to the other side of Metropolis, where Burnley College was located. She didn't like what she was hearing.

"Once again, that bulletin. Thaddeus Killgrave, the criminal genius who claims responsibility for infecting Superman with a deadly and highly contagious virus, is threatening to release the same disease into the world at noon today, according to a special edition of the *Daily Planet*. Editor Perry White—"

Lois gritted her teeth and switched off the radio. She'd just reached the Burnley campus, or what was left of it. The huge iron gates were closed, but they didn't have a chain on them.

By making his threat, Killgrave had raised the stakes. Now Lois wasn't just looking for a way to cure Superman of his disease. She was hoping to find a way to save the entire city.

Climbing out of her car, she crossed to the gates and pushed them open. They moved silently on well-oiled hinges. *Someone's been here recently,* she thought.

Lois drove into the grounds slowly, cautiously, gazing at the tall, decaying buildings set amid weed-infested lawns. Which of them would Killgrave use? Where would he have made his headquarters?

If he had been working with viruses, she

thought, he would have needed some research facilities. Finally she cruised past a more modern-looking building.

MEDICAL HALL, the sign out front read.

Lois drew to a stop and scanned the outside of the edifice for any hint of recent habitation but didn't see anything. Still, Killgrave was clever enough to hide his tracks.

She got out and headed up the walk to the front doors. Like the campus gates, there were no chains in place to keep anyone out. And when she opened the doors, they swung easily.

Again, a clue that someone had been here recently. But that someone didn't have to be Killgrave. *I'm still way out on a limb here,* the reporter thought. *And if Killgrave has his way, doomsday could be an hour away.*

The hallways were dark and foreboding, the only light filtering through the occasional window. As Lois negotiated the length of one corridor after another, her footfalls echoed sharply.

Then, just when Lois was wondering if she had barked up the wrong tree, she saw a pool of light in the distance. And it looked too diffuse to be sunlight through a window.

Eagerly Lois made her way to the end of the hall and peered around the corner at a perpendicular corridor. She blinked. The overhead fluorescent lights were on.

This has to be a sign, she thought. Why would

the electricity be on if nobody were here?

Slowly, carefully, she crept forward, listening for any telltale sounds. She didn't hear anything except a faint hum from the lights.

Lois opened the first door she came to and peered in. It was an observation gallery of some kind. It looked down on an operating theater, where she could see a spotless steel table, two state-of-the-art video cameras, and a couple of empty glass cages.

She had to get down there, she thought. If that's where the equipment was kept, that's where Killgrave's laboratory had to be.

Lois spent a few more minutes rummaging through the abandoned hallways, then found stairs down to the lower level. There were footprints in the dust here . . . small footprints—the kind someone of Killgrave's size might make, she thought triumphantly. It was the first proof she'd had that she was definitely on the right track.

Downstairs, things were different. The air had a sterile, almost filtered smell. When Lois opened the first door and walked in, she knew she'd found the right place.

This had to be Killgrave's lab, she realized, gazing across rows of glass cages. They all held dead white mice, some of them horribly disfigured. Lois had to look away to keep from getting sick.

A bookcase against the far wall held a series

of little vials. Lois picked up one, then another, then another, reading the labels.

VIRUS 77-G: FAILURE. VIRUS 77-H: FAILURE. VIRUS 78-A: FAILURE.

At least Killgrave had kept good records, she thought. But that was only natural for a man so thorough in his science.

Then again, his criminal activities had never been especially subtle. He'd always been so sure of success, he'd never bothered much to destroy incriminating evidence.

Besides, if he were successful in carrying out his latest threat, he would hardly have to worry about anyone bringing him to justice.

Lois tried not to think about that. She just searched vial after vial until she found what she was looking for.

VIRUS 152-B: SUCCESS.

The vial was marked with a date of three days ago . . . the day Superman had been infected, she realized. And next to it—

With a trembling hand, Lois picked up the next vial. VIRUS 152-B: ANTIDOTE. Her heart skipped a beat.

She'd been right. Killgrave had devised a cure. Otherwise, he would have been in as much jeopardy as anyone else exposed to the virus.

But did it work? Had it been tested?

There were six vials of the cure. She wrapped several in tissue and put them in her purse.

"One for Superman," Lois said softly, "and the

140

rest for S.T.A.R. Labs." They'd need it for analysis if they were going to synthesize and mass-produce an antiviral agent, she reasoned.

I just hope the stuff's for real, she thought as she rushed back out of the building. She had to get to S.T.A.R. Labs and Superman as quickly as possible.

Soaring over the city, conscious of the constraints imposed by his limited air supply, Superman felt a mounting sense of frustration. He'd tried all the obvious places in his hunt for Killgrave—the public plazas, zoos, skating rinks, and so on—but none of his hunches had paid off.

Banking to the right, he soared higher. He scanned the city with his telescopic vision, searching desperately for any sign of his nemesis. But there wasn't any.

Passing a clock tower, the Man of Steel noticed that it was a few minutes before noon. Time was running out, and he was no closer to his objective than when he started.

Think, he told himself. *What do you know about Killgrave? Is there some thread running through his crimes, some common denominator?*

In Superman's first encounter with Killgrave, the scientist had tried to use specially designed nuclear missiles to extort millions from Metropolis. The next time they met, Killgrave had created a robot juggernaut to bust himself out of Stryker's Island.

In fact, each time the madman showed up, it was with some super-sophisticated weapon of destruction. It was almost as if he had a—

—a fascination with such things?

Superman snapped his fingers. If he was lucky, he'd just hit the mother lode. Without another moment's hesitation, he headed crosstown at breakneck speed.

Killgrave got off the bus, had a leisurely meal at a sidewalk cafe by the seaport, then joined a group of tourists boarding the USS *Courageous*, a former destroyer that had been turned into a floating naval museum on Metropolis's West River.

As the long line shuffled up the gangplank, Killgrave studied the faces around him. They were worried. No doubt they had heard the news but decided to go on with their lives anyway.

After all, the citizens of Metropolis were a tough breed. They had endured threat after threat and lived to talk about it. More than likely, they believed they would live to talk about this one as well.

Killgrave snorted. Little did they know how wrong they were. Their little jaunt was about to end in horrible, agonizing death.

Of course, he would have no such problem. He had already taken the antidote.

The museum area included a few smaller

ships and a submarine, all of which were still in working order, but Killgrave thought the *Courageous* made the best location. He'd climb to the topmost deck, cross to the railing, and dump out his little vial full of virus.

He chuckled. It was almost a joke: the destroyer would be doing what it was built to do—destroy.

A smile slowly spread across his face. He had never realized how funny he could be.

Lois punched the number for S.T.A.R. Labs into her cellular phone as she wove rapidly through traffic. On the second ring, someone answered, and soon she had Kitty Faulkner on the line.

"Listen," she said, "I have a cure for Superman. Is he there?"

Kitty gasped. "You're sure it's a cure? How did you—?"

"No time for that now," Lois insisted. "Where's Superman?"

"Out searching for Killgrave," the woman told her.

Lois nodded; she might have expected that. "Is there any way you can contact him?" she asked.

"None," said Kitty. "We hadn't put a radio in his suit yet."

The reporter sighed. "All right, then. If he returns, let him know I've got a cure—but with any luck, I'll find him before you do. In the meantime, I have another job for you."

Quickly she imparted what she knew of Killgrave's secret lab at Burnley College.

"There are a lot more vials of the virus there, along with the cure—and a bunch of dead mice that might be infected. You'd better get a team in there to clean everything up."

"Will do," Kitty promised. "And Lois. . . good hunting!"

"Thanks," Lois said.

She glanced at the clock on her dashboard. Killgrave's deadline was fast approaching. They were almost out of time.

Lois leaned sideways and glanced up at the sky, hoping to see Superman flying among the skyscrapers of Metropolis. If she could somehow signal to him. . .

Killgrave could see the Scarsdale Tower perfectly from the deck of the ship. He could also see the clock set into it, its hands slowly and inexorably moving toward high noon.

High noon—the perfect time for death, he thought with a little laugh. It had a certain finality to it, just like something out of a movie.

Leaning forward, Killgrave looked down at the crowds milling about the big guns below him. Two minutes more, he thought.

He smiled and waved to the people below, and to his surprise a couple of kids noticed him and waved back. With his small size, they probably thought he was one of them. Little did they know.

The minute hand on the clock moved another tick. One minute. Sixty small seconds.

Killgrave began to have some nagging doubts. After all, this was it—there would be no turning back. He was about to doom not just the city, but potentially all of mankind.

Then again, what good had any of them ever done for him? What did he need people for, anyway?

Victory was victory. And wasn't winning all that really counted in the end? Victory at any cost? That, and his revenge on the late, great Superman.

The virus wouldn't hurt Killgrave in the least. But it would destroy Superman's world, and all those in it who worshiped him.

He raised the vial, preparing to unleash his plague. All he had to do was remove the cork, turn the vial over, and spill out the contents. The winds and time would do the rest.

The clock's minute hand ticked over.

Church bells began to chime all over the city.

Killgrave took a deep breath and started to remove the cork from the vial—but before he could, a white blur whizzed past him at superspeed, and a sudden gust of wind knocked him back a half step.

Killgrave gaped at his suddenly empty hand.

The vial—it was gone. Realization set in. That blur . . . Superman!

Looking up, he saw the Man of Steel circling back—holding the vial protectively before him, cradling it in his hands. Killgrave could see a huge, relieved grin on his face through the containment suit's faceplate.

"How—?" the scientist began.

Superman drew up in front of him and hovered. "At the last minute," he said, "I remembered your fascination with weapons of mass destruction. Once I'd scanned the armory and Fort Bridwell to no avail, I took a chance this was your next logical destination."

"You're too clever for your own good," Killgrave snarled. "You still don't have the cure—and you never will!"

"The police are on their way," said Superman, seemingly unperturbed. Or was he just putting on a face for the public? "The party's over, Killgrave, whether you like it or not."

Killgrave lowered his eyes, as if resigned to his fate. But his mind was racing ahead, trying, then discarding, one escape plan after another.

There had to be a way to turn defeat into victory. If only he could get Superman to drop the vial and release the virus . . .

Or, he thought, if he could release the virus trapped inside Superman's containment suit!

In one quick motion, he whipped out the tiny laser he always carried now and fired. He didn't have to be fancy; all he had to do was hit Superman. Head, chest, foot—it didn't matter where. Even the smallest puncture would do the trick.

The laser caught Superman across the right arm, opening a two-inch rent in the containment suit.

"That's it!" Killgrave howled in triumph. "The virus is free, Superman—and there's nothing you can do about it!"

The Man of Steel grabbed the torn cloth with one hand, pressing it closed. He'd moved quickly—had the virus escaped? Killgrave couldn't be sure.

Flying backward as fast as he could, Superman retreated from the laser. Killgrave took aim and fired again but missed. Now aware of the danger, his enemy was effecting evasive maneuvers.

Killgrave snarled and kept on firing.

CHAPTER FIFTEEN

Frantic to keep the virus from becoming airborne, Superman avoided bolt after bolt from Killgrave's laser by ascending out of range. Finally he noticed the naval museum's submarine. It wasn't an ideal refuge, but it was airtight and might do the trick.

Quickly he flew over to it. The submarine wasn't open to the public, but its hatch was ajar.

He ducked inside, slammed the hatch shut over his head, then began closing all the air locks. It was his only hope for containing the virus now that his suit had been breached.

Then he let out the breath he'd been holding, and drew in another one. Finally he pulled the headpiece off his containment suit.

He stared at the tiny vial in his hand. It was hard to believe it held a virus that could wipe out the entire population of Metropolis. Or that, despite his best efforts, the city he had sworn to protect and all its occupants might already have been exposed. What was worse, he was helpless in here.

All his adult life he tried to help people, to save lives. Now it seemed he might have paved the way for a plague of nightmarish proportions.

If Killgrave had another vial, the fate of Metropolis was sealed. And its champion couldn't do anything about it.

* * *

With Superman ensconced in the submarine, Killgrave thought about trying to get away. But police cars were already gathering at the entrance to the museum, and there was no way he could get past them.

Worse, his plan to infect the city had failed. Thanks to Superman, Metropolis would be spared the plague he'd had in mind for it.

Still, Killgrave was happy—happier than he had been his whole life. Ducking behind the rail of the *Courageous*, he propped his back against it and crowed gleefully.

After all, Killgrave wasn't the only one trapped and alone, likely to spend the rest of his life in prison. Superman was imprisoned too, in that sub. And if he ever tried to leave, he'd be taking a chance on infecting the whole city with his virus.

It was wonderful. He had turned the Man of Steel's story of sacrifice and success into one of tragedy. Finally, Superman would know what it was like to live without friends, without true companionship.

Without love.

Killgrave laughed again, even louder than before. Once, he would have said that he and Superman had little in common. Now, they were very much in the same boat . . .

. . . abandoned and alone.

As the clocks began to chime noon, bright flashes of light lit up the sky over the West River.

"Laser bolts!" Lois Lane said, watching from her car window.

She knew the target had to be Superman. Unless she missed her guess, the Man of Steel had found Killgrave. But was he in time?

Lois pulled on to the West Side Highway and drove as fast as traffic would allow. She'd come within a hundred yards of the floating naval museum before she realized the police were diverting traffic onto the side streets.

Pay dirt, she thought. She pulled off the road onto the hard shoulder and parked. She didn't care if they ticketed or towed her. She had to get the cure to Superman.

As Lois started to run toward the destroyer, a young cop moved to intercept her.

"Where do you think you're going?" he demanded, blocking her way. "Get back in your car!"

"I have the cure for Superman!" Lois began.

"Yeah, and I'm Jonas Salk. Move back, lady—now!"

An older officer came jogging over. "That's Lois Lane from the *Daily Planet*," he said to the younger cop. "She's the one who's always getting those scoops from Superman. If she says she's got a cure, it might be true."

"Yeah?" the younger cop said. "Well, in that case—"

"Where is he?" Lois asked the older policeman. "Can I see him?"

"He's here," the officer said, jerking a thumb at the grounds of the naval museum, "but it's going to be a problem getting the cure to him." He explained how Superman had locked himself inside the submarine.

Lois swallowed. If Killgrave's laser had opened a hole in Superman's containment suit . . .

"I'll take it to him," she said.

The two cops looked at her. "*You* will?" the older one echoed. "Do you know what that means—?" he began.

"Not much," she told him, "if the cure works. And if not . . ." She shrugged. "You want to make an omelet, you've got to break some eggs."

The older cop swallowed. "Okay," he decided. "If you're sure…"

Lois nodded. "I am."

"This way," he said.

Taking her arm, he led her through the line of police to a gangplank, the one that gave access to the sub.

Commissioner Henderson was already there, overseeing the placement of a squad of police marksmen. By then the crowds had been cleared out of the place—though Killgrave, apparently, was still at large.

Lois followed the sharpshooters' gaze. It was trained on the top deck of the *Courageous*. That's where Killgrave must have been, she realized, though the scientist was now nowhere in sight. He was probably hiding behind the rail, his laser still in hand. And who knew what else.

Henderson's brow furrowed at the sight of Lois. "This is no place for a reporter," he snarled, advancing on her. "I'm afraid you'll have to—"

"I've got the cure," she said.

Henderson stopped. He looked surprised. "You're not just saying that to get a story, are you? Because, so help me, Miss Lane—"

"It's no ploy," she told him, taking out the vial she carried. "It came out of Killgrave's lab. And right now, I'd say it's our best hope."

Henderson looked at the vial, then at Lois again. "Maybe our only hope. Apparently Killgrave opened a hole in Superman's suit. The virus may have got out before he could close it again."

Lois nodded. "I heard. That makes it all the more important that you let me give this to him."

The commissioner frowned. "I could have one of my men do it. They get paid to risk their lives."

The reporter shook her head. Though she couldn't say it, Superman—Clark—was her responsibility. She would be the one to bring him the cure, no one else.

Henderson stepped aside, somewhat reluctantly. "He's all yours, then."

Suppressing a shudder, Lois set one foot on the gangplank. Then the other. Crossing over to the sub, she approached the hatch.

She was assailed by doubts. What if the

antidote didn't work? What if Killgrave had labeled it wrong? Or just deluded himself into thinking it would cure the virus?

Putting such thoughts aside, Lois advanced to the hatch, twisted the handle, and popped it open. Taking a deep breath, she ducked inside and pulled it shut after her with a loud clang.

It was dark inside the sub. Dark and musty. Lois groped her way forward through the gloom, careful to keep a good grip on the vial.

After a moment, she called out, "Superman?"

Suddenly he appeared in front of her, a fearful expression on his shadowed face. He raised his hands for her to go back, and Lois realized he was afraid—not for himself, but for her.

Superman shook his head, as if the sight of her was torture to him. "Get out of here!" he rasped. "Don't come any closer—you'll get infected!"

It tore her heart out to see him this way. But there was no turning back now.

Lois held up the vial. "I have the cure. At least, I think I do."

Superman stared at it. "Where did you get that? Not from S.T.A.R. Labs?"

"I found Killgrave's secret lab," she explained. "He was holed up in the medical building at the old Burnley College campus."

"You still shouldn't have come," he said. "Now that you've been exposed, the virus can kill you."

Lois reached for his face, traced the line of his

jaw with her fingertips. If she was wrong, if the cure didn't work . . . at least she had been able to touch him one last time.

"It won't," Lois said hopefully. "Not if we take the antidote together."

Superman smiled. "You first," he told her.

Obediently she twisted the cork out of the vial, took a deep breath, and raised it to her lips. She drank half of it and offered the rest to her fiancé.

Superman drained what was left in the vial.

"Now what?" asked Lois.

He took her hands in his. "Now we wait."

Jimmy Olsen stood at the front of the crowd outside the museum grounds, waiting to see what would happen. It had been three hours since Superman had foiled Killgrave's attempt to murder everyone in Metropolis—but the scientist was still holed up on the top deck of the *Courageous*.

And Superman, now accompanied by Lois, was holed up, too—in the belly of the museum's submarine. According to the police Jimmy had talked to, Lois had supposedly brought an antidote onto the sub. Now everyone was standing around, waiting to see what would happen.

Jimmy bit his lip. To everyone else, maybe, Superman and Lois were strangers. To him, they were friends. He hoped with all his heart that they would come out of this alive.

And the rest of Metropolis, too.

Abruptly he heard a clanging noise, and the hatch of the submarine popped open. Instinctively raising his camera, Jimmy brought the scene into focus and prepared to shoot.

For a moment, nothing happened. Then Superman stepped out onto the deck—and though he was wearing the containment suit, he no longer wore the helmet that went with it. His hands were exposed as well.

And he was smiling—as if he'd just heard the best joke in the world. Bending down, he extended a hand to Lois and helped her out. Not unexpectedly, she was smiling, too.

Jimmy began snapping photos, grinning happily along with them. Obviously, the antidote had worked. Using his microscopic vision, Superman must have determined that he was cured.

Then, as if he had remembered something deadly important, the Man of Steel raised his gaze to the top deck of the *Courageous*—and took off like a shot. Inwardly, Jimmy cheered him on as he re-aimed his camera.

Seeing his adversary, Killgrave came out of hiding and blasted him with one laser beam after another. The beams sliced up the containment suit, but Superman himself was unharmed.

Then, when he had demonstrated to Killgrave just how futile it was to come after the Man of Steel with a few measly laser beams, Superman darted in and grabbed the weapon. With a flexing of his fingers, he reduced it to debris. Then he grabbed Killgrave by the collar of his jacket and brought him down to earth.

"Don't worry," Superman cried to the police as he descended with the scientist. "He doesn't have any other vials on him—I checked."

"What about the *first* vial?" asked Commissioner Henderson. "Did any of that stuff get into the air?"

"Apparently not," said Superman. He turned Killgrave over to the cops. "Though I'm going to inspect more closely to make sure."

The crowd began to cheer. Jimmy lowered his camera and smiled. Superman was back—and nobody could be happier to see him.

EPILOGUE

Clark winced a little as he played back the dozens of messages his parents had left on his voice mail at work. He picked up his phone and dialed their number. His mother answered on the first ring.

"Mom?" he said. "It's—"

"Clark!" she blurted. "We were so worried. All those news reports said—"

"I know, I know," he said. "But at least you had Lois to give you the real story."

His father picked up the extension. "We're just glad everything worked out. We watched the whole thing at the submarine live on CNN."

"I'll come see you tonight and give you all the details," Clark promised. "I'm at the *Planet* now."

"Okay," his mother said. "I'll make an apple pie."

Clark felt a twinge of gratitude. He had thought he might never see his parents again, much less taste his mother's apple pie.

"Thanks, Mom," he told her. "See you tonight." He hung up.

"New edition's here!" a copyboy shouted, bringing a stack of papers hot off the presses into the bull pen.

Clark joined the crowd of *Planet* employees and took one. The headline read SUPERMAN IS BACK!

The story told of Killgrave's defeat at the hands of Superman. It also mentioned that environmental tests had shown no evidence of the virus in the air—though if the disease ever turned up again, they had the cure on hand.

At Lois's insistence, the article's byline contained both their names: Lois Lane and Clark Kent. Nonetheless, he knew Lois had done all the work on this one—both as a reporter and as a friend. It was her courage and loyalty that had turned the tide.

Superman would get the credit for taking down Killgrave and for stopping the crime wave that had ravaged the city. But in Clark's mind, there was only one *real* hero here—and he was looking at her.

Lois, on the other hand, was looking over the story. Finally she glanced up at Clark and smiled. "Nice going, partner. We pulled it off again."

"In more ways than one," he replied. Clark took her hand. He felt the warmth of her skin and appreciated the sensation more than ever before. "Thanks, Lois."

"Anytime."

Their banter was that of a couple of professionals, reveling in the satisfaction of a job well done. But behind those words, behind the casual expressions, there was much more to it.

They had almost lost each other. They both knew that. Fate had been kind to them this time, but it could just as easily have gone the other way.

It reminded Clark once again how lucky he was to have Lois on his side. Silently, he promised never to forget that.

Suddenly Perry White came out of his office, picked one of the papers off the stack, and perused the headlines.

"Good story, Lois, Clark," he said, nodding to them. "But next time, check in from time to time, will you? I don't like it when my ace reporters drop out of sight for three days."

"But you have to admit we delivered the goods," Lois countered, covering for Clark as always. "Everyone kept swearing us to secrecy. And then there was that trip to Maine—"

Perry held up a hand. "Don't worry about it . . . this time."

The phone on his desk began to ring. Clark picked it up. "Kent here," he said.

"Clark!" a familiar voice replied. "This is Keith DeCann from *Newstime*. You're a tough guy to track down!"

"Uh, hi, Keith," Clark said, glancing at Lois. "What's up?"

"I still owe you that check for a hundred smackeroos. Who gets the big bucks?"

Clark grinned at Lois. "S.T.A.R. Labs," he said. "I owe them one." And then, noticing curious stares from everyone else in the newsroom, he added, "We all do."

About the Author

When roused from one of his frequent and enduring daydreams of a world where baseball players never go on strike and White Castle hamburgers grow on trees, M. J. Friedman will admit to being the author of nineteen science fiction and fantasy books, among them a great many Star Trek and Star Trek: The Next Generation bestsellers.

When he's not writing—a condition that lately occurs with the frequency of Halley's Comet—Friedman enjoys sailing, jogging, and spending time with his adorable wife Joan and two equally adorable clones . . . er, sons. He's quick to note that no matter how many Friedmans you may know, he's probably not related to any of them.